# Keys to
# the Heart

# Keys to the Heart

## a romance

JENNIFER ROSE

Distributed in 2015 by Open Road Distribution
345 Hudson Street
New York, NY 10014
www.openroadmedia.com

*For Ida*

# Keys to
# the Heart

# Chapter 1

MEG DUNCAN looked at the enormous bed and laughed.

It never failed. The law of inverse bed ratios, she and Don called it. Check into a hotel together, and what would they find in their room? Skimpy twin beds, decisively separated by a night table with sharp corners and scratchy hardware, the whole setup clearly designed for eight hours of chaste, solitary sleep. But check into a hotel singly, and the bed in question was unfailingly of playground proportions, a mocking invitation to frolic until dawn.

Tipping the gray-haired bellman, Meg smilingly endured his admonition to have a nice evening. As the door closed behind him, she stuck her tongue out at the bed and glumly contemplated the prospect of a long night of tossing and pillow hugging.

Oh, well. She'd manage. There was really no need to get dramatic. A number of forced separations during her ten-year marriage had taught her all too well how to lull herself to sleep when Don wasn't there to put his arms around her and pull her over the brink.

She would unpack, have a quick shower, swim a dozen laps in the hotel pool, dine on a seafood salad and a light Bloody Mary, and bring her briefcase to bed. If the exercise and the vodka didn't knock her out, another perusal of *U.S. v. Hernandez* would surely do her in. Or if all the tricks failed and she had a bumpy night, she could always sleep through the daylong meeting scheduled to begin at nine the next morning.

Like her husband, Don, Meg was an attorney. They had both worked for the Department of Justice, specializing in immigration problems, in the decade since they'd both graduated from law school. Based in Washington, D.C., the Duncans were frequently posted to other parts of the country to advise local and federal law enforcement officials. Sometimes they were posted separately, sometimes together. They had happily shared the autumn just past in California, helping to cope with the annual influx of illegal migrant workers coming north for the grape harvest. No sooner had she and Don returned and taken the dust covers off the furniture in their Georgetown apartment, then she had been packed off to Miami for a week-long colloquium on the never-ending tide of aliens flowing up onto the Florida shores.

Taking swim togs and light cotton dresses from her well-seasoned, soft leather suitcase, Meg had to concede that there were worse places to be in early December than Miami. That afternoon the skies back home had offered an unappealing precipitation somewhere between frozen rain and liquid snow, delaying her takeoff from National by half an hour and undermining her usual calm attitude toward flying. She wasn't sure that her presence in Miami would shed much light on Florida's immigration problems—she was of the opinion that very little was ever accomplished by a meeting of more than two minds—but at least she'd be able to freshen her California tan and bring a brighter body home to Don's winter.

That was the great bonus of traveling singly: every separation meant a reunion. Unlike some couples they knew, who seemed to be choking on an overdose of togetherness, the Duncans were constantly rediscovering each other. Meg shivered with anticipation as she thought ahead to Friday night. Don would feverishly undress her, exclaiming over each cherished, well-remembered inch of flesh. If her skin was darker or paler, her belly flatter or rounder, her hair a millimeter longer or maybe altered by foreign scissors, he would invariably notice, invariably approve. He would run possessive hands over her whole body, reclaiming it as his, welcoming it home.

Sighing, Meg reached into her suitcase and carefully withdrew the folded tennis dress she would probably not get to use this week. She laid the brief white garment on the bed and spread it open to reveal a small photograph in a green leather frame. She placed the photo on a chest of drawers, angling it to reflect in the vast horizontal mirror above. Don would have laughed at her for being so greedy—wanting the reflected picture as well as the real one. He would have understood, though. The picture was four—no, five—years old, and their colleague Andrea Roberts, an avid photographer, had shot many successors; but this remained unrivaled as a perfect portrait of the Duncan marriage.

The photograph had been snapped just after Meg and Don had won a round-robin mixed doubles tennis tournament, catching Don in the act of swinging Meg up off her feet in an exuberant victory hug. Both the Duncans were wearing white shirts, decidedly rumpled, and shorts. Their straight, collar-length brown hair was in similar disarray. At first glance they had an air of innocent, all-American wholesomeness; they might have been brother and sister. A second glance caught the deliberate thrust of Meg's breasts against Don's chest—the sensual gleam in his eyes. The photographer seemed to have perceived that the true celebration of their victory would come in bed that night.

It had. Meg still so vividly recalled the quality of their lovemaking after the tournament that now, five years later, she let out a little gasp and thudded down onto the solitary king-size hotel bed. Bodies honed all day to perfect partnership had moved that night in a single, flawless rhythm, answering each other's needs only to provoke new needs . . . on and on through the spiraling night.

She and Don were partners; that was their secret. In the courts and on the courts, in bed, everywhere. They were the two halves of a puzzle; they were eggs and bacon; they were subject and predicate; they were light and shadow—you name it. Partners. The tensions of their work and their forced separations only confirmed the profundity of that precious link.

They had married within weeks of their first meeting. New graduates of different law schools, they had been the two low-ranking employees in the Immigration and Naturalization Service of the mighty Justice Department. A decision to team up at work had escalated almost immediately into a desire to team up across the board. Every passing year had underscored the wisdom of the first hot, instinctual draw they'd felt toward each other.

Meg forced her mind away from the past, her eyes away from the photograph. Really, she was getting too sentimental for words. Maybe it was the fine fall she'd spent with Don, or the thirty-fifth birthday she'd celebrated just after Thanksgiving. In any case, something was making this separation feel different from those of the past. This time around she didn't feel worldly and important; she felt just plain lonely.

She looked at the telephone, then away from it. As much as she longed to hear Don's voice, she didn't want to inflict her present mood on him. The Duncans were deeply responsive to each other's feelings. Sometimes when one of them was down, the other could change the mood to up; but more often the down one ruined the up one's day. Having Don blue in Georgetown wouldn't make her any less blue in Miami. She'd snap herself out of this and *then* call him.

Meg got into the shower before she could weaken. Adjusting the multiple nozzles, she created an instant spa, hydromassaging her tense muscles. The Coconut Grove Hotel didn't stint on luxury, she had to admit, as she groaned happily under the pounding water. The organizers of the immigration conference claimed to have chosen the hotel because it was a mere twenty minutes from the airport and ten minutes from downtown Miami, but Meg suspected that the amenities of the new twenty-one-story tower hotel were more to the point.

Dressed in a cotton robe, standing on her private terrace overlooking the pale angles of the Miami skyline to the north and the limpid blues of Biscayne Bay straight before her, Meg actually felt guilty and cross. The American public was picking up the tab for this conference. A head-by-head vote across the nation might support the basic policies of the Immigration and Naturalization Service, but she didn't kid herself that Jane Q. Citizen would think the enforcers of those policies needed balconies.

"But what about all the Saturday nights I pored over casebooks while you were at the movies?" she retorted to her mythical critic. "And what about the fact that my husband is eight hundred miles away? Really, Ms. Citizen, I'd rather be up north in my humble abode with my own sweet Don than here in this solitary splendor."

She was distracted from her little scenario by the slow, graceful sweeps and swoops of a sailboat on the bay below her. She had no use for boats herself. Even thinking too much about boats had an awful effect on her stomach. But there was something eternally touching about the sight of a lone boat making its way home to its harbor as the sun was starting to sink. She could almost sense the healthy weariness of the sailors below her as their day drew to a close. She could almost feel their longing for fresh clothes, frosted drinks, and a big dinner. Too bad she could also feel the nausea that would surely be hers if she'd spent the day at sea.

As the boat moored, she could see its occupants—a young, blond couple in their twenties or thirties, wearing cutoff jeans and oversized shirts, colorful Shetland sweaters knotted around their shoulders. Inevitably she thought of her beloved Uncle Win. He was her late mother's older brother, her only surviving blood relative. A few years ago he'd plundered his bulging stock portfolio and bought a marina full of houseboats—or floating homes, as he called them—down in Key West. When queried as to why he had made the highly unlikely purchase, he invariably replied, "Because they were there."

In fact, he had a passionate fondness for water. He liked to say that he'd spent the first nine months of his existence floating, and he was going to spend the last years of his life in the same happy condition. He was forever trying to persuade Meg and Don to give up "the pursuit of anxiety" and take a long rest on one of his houseboats when it was between rentals. The Duncans were fond enough of Win to have taken two long vacations in Key West to be near him, and to have made plans to spend the coming Christmas holidays there. But when they visited him, they always stayed on dry, unmoving ground, thank you—typically in a guest house with skinny twin beds!

Meg's assignment to Miami had been such a last-minute business that she hadn't had time to write Uncle Win. Insisting that the absence of a telephone was a privilege, not a deprivation, he relied on his post-office box for communication with the world to the north of the Seven Mile Bridge. The Coconut Grove Hotel was a good three-hour drive from Key West, and of course she and Don would be down in the Keys for Christmas in just three weeks, but she felt she had to let Win know she was in the sovereign state of Florida. Maybe he'd hop onto one of the propjets that flew between Key West and. Miami and join her for dinner one evening during her brief sojourn.

Hmm—quarter to six. Chances were he was sitting at his favorite haunt, the Half Shell Raw Bar down on the shrimp docks, having a beer and a basketful of spicy conch fritters. Impulsively Meg went to the bedside telephone, rang Information in Key West, and got the number for the Half Shell.

When the bartender answered against a cozy clatter of sounds, Meg would have sworn she could smell the conch fritters. However lavish the menu might be at Horatio's, atop the hotel, she doubted her dinner would hold a candle to the rough but sublime fare at the Half Shell. A moment later all thoughts of food fled her mind. The bartender said he hadn't seen Win Carruthers in three or four days and, come to think of it, he was a little worried about that. Meg instantly adopted her crispest tone of voice—what Don called her courtroom staccato. In words that brooked no possibility of refusal, she announced that she was Win's niece—and an attorney with the Department of Justice—and she wanted the bartender to drop everything and get himself over to the marina where the *Agualinda* was moored, and then report back to her.

Although she and the bartender assured each other that Win was probably just fine, or maybe had a cold, Meg knew that the young man at the other end of the wire was as anxious as she was. Win was an original—an eccentric, if you liked—but within his self-designed framework he had patterns and habits just as conventional people did. And Win didn't get colds. Anything so mild would be regarded as an insult to his body. If he was sick, it was serious.

Asking the hotel operator to page her at the swimming pool if a call came, Meg scrambled into her blue-and-green bathing suit. She stopped in front of the mirror and made a face. The design of the swimsuit was supposed to draw attention away from her generous bosom, but she didn't think the manufacturer had totally succeeded in that ambition. To her eyes she was all curves and cleavage. Never mind the great strides the world had taken in its attitudes about sex and sexuality. There were still men who thought that big breasts were a statement, an invitation, not simply a fact like ears and toes. It wasn't as if Meg had gone in for silicone injections or bosom-swelling exercises. In fact, the opposite was true. As an embarrassed teenager she'd bought bras a size too small in hopes of squelching her mammary development. As an adult she dressed as discreetly as possible.

Oh, well. If anyone got too interested in her, she'd just turn over, revealing a boyish bottom that was bound to disappoint any curve-lover.

Meg drew on a terry robe thoughtfully supplied by the hotel management and made her way out to the elevator. Crossing beneath the lobby and bar through a special passageway, she emerged at poolside a few minutes later, smiling with pleasure. The pool area was deserted, save for a small girl and her parents. Palms waved invitingly behind the turquoise rectangle of water. As she shrugged off her robe, the warm air of early evening settled around her shoulders like a mantle. Through the big glass windows in front of her, she could see people having drinks at small tables, their head bent toward each other in conversation. They might be new lovers, or people making business deals, or maybe some of the immigration honchos she'd be meeting the next morning. Right now she didn't care. She pulled a chaise longue close to the pool and stretched out on it, deciding to let her body enjoy the warm, swirling air before she plunged it into the cool, refreshing water.

Meg closed her eyes and sank into reverie. She indulged in a rare flight of fancy, letting herself pretend that she was waiting for Don to come down from their room and join her. Any second he would sneak up behind her, slide warm hands down over her pronounced collarbones—

She sat up, yelping, her eyes flying open, as cold hands dribbled water down her chest.

"Hi," said the culprit. It was the small, blond girl Meg had glimpsed earlier. "My name is Calliope. Some people say it sort of like cantaloupe, but that's dumb. *Ca-LIE-o-pee*. Four syllables. She was a Greek Muse, and she had a beautiful voice, and I do too. I know eighteen million hundred songs. I'm five and a half," she added breathlessly, "but I'm very smart for my age. Do you have a little girl?"

"No," was all Meg could say.

Calliope leaned her small swimsuited figure over the arm of Meg's chair, shedding droplets of cold water. She began to deflate the yellow plastic apparatus she wore on each upper arm. Meg cast a longing look toward the girl's parents, but they had just unfolded a portable back-gammon board and seemed not at all inclined to remind their darling that strangers sometimes liked to be left in peace.

"Do you have a little boy?" Calliope asked. She dropped the yellow plastic things to the ground and gave them a disdainful kick.

"I don't have any children," Meg said. She refrained from adding, "And you confirm the brilliance of my decision." Instead she asked, "What are those yellow devices you're brutalizing?"

"They're my water wings," Calliope said. "They're kind of babyish, but Melinda and Jorge insist." She gave the sulky sort of look Meg had seen on the faces of grown-ups at cocktail parties, usually when discussing some imperfection of their spouses. "Of course I don't need them if I have someone in the water with me, so why don't you come in?"

Meg was hot enough now to be longing for the water, but she had a dozen brisk laps in mind, not horseplay with a precocious five-year-old.

"Why don't you ask your parents?" she suggested.

"They just started another match," Calliope said. "That means seven games, unless someone gets doubled. Melinda never resigns when Jorge doubles her, and sometimes she really gets trounced. I think backgammon's a dumb game."

"Me too," Meg said, beginning to feel some kinship with the talk-ative child. She mustered a tentative smile, taking in Calliope's huge turquoise eyes and improbably long lashes.

At that moment the mother turned from the board, swinging a long pelt of blond hair across her perfectly tanned back. She looked at Meg and Calliope and gave a little wave, as though signaling her approval of the friendship.

"You see?" Calliope said in a sad, wise voice that knifed through Meg's heart. "They don't care."

"Of course they care," Meg said automatically. She knew very little about parents and children—she and Don had naturally drifted into friendships with other couples who had chosen not to have children— but she was lawyer enough to know it was a mistake to leap to conclusions about *any* relationship when you had scanty evidence. For all she knew, the backgammon-playing couple had never before turned their backs on their daughter. At least they'd brought her to Florida with them instead of leaving her at home, wherever home was, in the care of someone else.

"Where do you come from?" Meg asked.

Instead of answering, Calliope delivered one more defiant kick to the water wings next to Meg's chair, then made a sudden dash for the pool. Meg sat frozen for a disbelieving moment, then leaped to her feet as Calliope started down the steps at the deep end of the pool.

"Look, Mama," the child called out excitedly. Giving an exuberant wave in the direction of her unseeing parents, she lost her footing, and her bubbling laughter gave way to a panicky shriek. Meg made a flat dive into the pool just as the child disappeared below the surface, her hair floating Ophelia-like above her.

"I was drowning," Calliope shouted between hiccups and sobs, as Meg scooped her up and out.

"You weren't drowning, but you could have, and if you ever go in the pool again without your wings, I'll—I'll—" Meg broke off as the child's parents came running toward Calliope and Meg with towels and exclamations, expressions of concern on their faces.

"Baby girl!" The mother swung her dripping daughter out of Meg's arms.

"I was drowning," Calliope wailed, clinging to the woman.

The tall, dark, perfectly lean father briefly tousled the child's fair hair. "Don't carry on, Cal. You're fine." He had a faint accent, which Meg's practiced ear identified as Brazilian. Turning to her, he made the obligatory speech. "We are Jorge and Melinda Figueiro. How can we ever thank you?" His eyes focused flagrantly on Meg's bosom.

"By giving your daughter swimming lessons," Meg snapped, turning away. Shaking with anger, relief, and leftover adrenaline, she started back toward her chaise longue. As she sank down onto it, pulling on sunglasses and facing away from the family threesome, an unexpected wave of loneliness washed over her. If only Don were there! But would even Don be able to erase the unnameable ache that engulfed her? For a panicky moment she seemed to be staring into some terrifying void; then her own laughter pulled her back. She was just plain homesick for her husband, that was all. "Don't carry on," she instructed herself, in the words of Calliope's father.

She heard the preliminary crackle of the public address system, and she went on alert, her thoughts swinging to Key West and her Uncle Win.

"Telephone call for Meg Duncan. Mrs. Duncan, telephone, please."

Meg bolted toward the white wall-phone near the entrance to the passageway leading back to the hotel proper. "Hello? Meg Duncan here."

"Mrs. Duncan? Hi. This is Flip Peterson at the Half Shell. Boy, am I glad you sent me over to the *Agualinda.*"

"Yes?" Meg urged him, over the thumping of her heart.

"It looks to me like pneumonia. My aunt had it once. Win says he won't go to the hospital. He doesn't even want a doctor. He says he wants a six-pack of Rolling Rock, two dozen conch fritters, and your husband and you."

# Chapter 2

O F COURSE I'LL COME," Don said instantly when Meg called him with the news. "I love the old character, and, even if I didn't, I know you love him and I love you. I'll see if I can get a flight out of National tonight, though it looks like something damn close to an ice storm outside my window. You check the scheduled flights to Key West, and if nothing's flying late tonight, try the charters. I'll square every-thing with the office for both of us, though I suppose you'll have to talk to the conference people, too. Sorry, darling," he added, and Meg could see him smiling tenderly into the phone. "Am I being too take-charge? You see what happens to me—eight hours without you, and I forget there's another person in the world who's as smart as I am. You having fun down there? Aside from worrying your head off about Win?"

"Very nice. I saved a five-year-old from drowning while her par-ents played backgammon, and now I'm trying to figure out how to get her away from them."

There was a pause, and then Don said lightly, "Don't get too much sun, darling. It makes you dangerous. Well, I ought to start making phone calls. Love you a lot. Do you have a great big double bed?"

"Of course." Meg laughed. "I'm sprawled all over it this minute, and there's still half an acre to go."

Hanging up, she gazed longingly at the phone for a minute before deciding she'd better have a shower pronto. If she hung around much longer, in her wet swimsuit in the air-conditioned room, there would be a second candidate for pneumonia in the family.

She was toweling herself dry when Don called back to report that National was iced in for the night, but flights were expected to resume in the morning.

"I'd better go down to Key West on my own tonight," Meg decided. "Assuming I can find someone to fly me."

"Oh, there's probably some big dope dealer with a Lear jet who'll let you hitch a ride," Don said cheerfully. "Just make sure he knows you're not a narc."

"Thanks a lot," Meg said. "If I can't change Win's mind about going to the hospital, I suppose I'll have to stay on the *Agualinda* tonight. I'd better pick up a giant-economy-size bottle of Dramamine on my way to the airport. I'll book us a room at a guest house for tomorrow night and give you a call in the morning to let you know what's what. If I miss you, I'll leave a message with Flip at the Half Shell. Am I being too take-charge? It's just—"

"Funny girl," Don said. "Miss you, darling. I wish I could be there tonight. What are you wearing?"

"A towel."

Don groaned. "That's unfair. Damn this storm. Remember when it used to be kind of exciting to spend a night apart?"

"I know," Meg said. "I was thinking about it earlier. What's happening to us, Don?" she added in mock terror. "We're getting soft."

"I'm not entirely soft at the moment."

"Talk about unfair!" Meg sighed into the phone. "Save it for me. I'd better hang up," she went on, "or I'll start to cry. Do you think Win is going to be okay?"

"He's a tough old buzzard," Don reassured her. "On the other hand, darling, if he really won't let a doctor near him . . . Antibiotics make all the difference in pneumonia. I'll call Ed Roberts tonight and ask his advice, though I suppose it means he'll start bugging me about coming in for a checkup."

"Oh, please do," Meg said. "And if Andrea answers, tell her I have her photograph with me—as usual. See you tomorrow, my love."

A quick call to Air Florida brought the information that they had a flight to Key West at eight o'clock and could book a seat for her. Hurriedly repacking the suitcase she'd just unpacked, she left out the all-important photograph, only to discover it during her last-minute room check. She put it in her pale leather shoulder bag. An hour later, as the Cessna sevenseater thrust into the star-spangled sky, she pulled the photograph out and clutched it for a talisman. *Let Win be okay*, she prayed silently.

"Fear of flying?" asked her seatmate, a silver-haired man who looked to be in his late fifties.

"Not at all," Meg said. "I love to fly. And I like small planes best of all—it's fun to actually be able to see all the controls."

"Next best thing to being in control," the man said dryly. He looked at the photograph with open curiosity. "Your brother?"

"My husband," Meg said.

"You going to the Keys to join him or get away from him?"

Meg stared silently at the stranger for a moment, lifting her eyebrows slightly. "Is that question material, counselor?"

The man roared with laughter. "How the hell did you know I'm a lawyer?"

"Because I'm one too."

"Oh yeah? Let me guess." He looked her over, seemingly assessing the straight, almost sculptural brown hair that she wore parted on one side, the wide-set brown eyes under unplucked brows, the firm, determined chin. "Wall Street, I'd guess. Or one of the big corporations."

"Department of Justice," Meg said crisply. "And you? My turn to guess. A trial lawyer."

"You got it. Victor Green for the defense." He held out a large hand.

"Victor Green?" Meg was too startled to offer her own hand. "I just finished reading your brief for *U.S. v. Hernandez*. I'm Meg Duncan," she added a bit lamely, remembering to complete the handshake.

"Meg Duncan? And that's Don?" Victor Green pointed to the photograph on Meg's lap. "Meg Duncan of the Dauntless Duncans, keepers of the flame, scourge of the alien enemy? Aren't you supposed to be back in Coconut Grove with the other bigwigs, figuring out how to make sure no one ever becomes an American without being born here?"

"That's hardly how I see my work," Meg said stiffly. She stared gloomily at the seatback in front of her. At any other time she would have welcomed a clashing of minds with Victor Green, probably the best immigration lawyer in the country. But she hardly needed more tension at the moment.

To her surprise, her silver-haired seatmate reached over and patted her hand, chortling loudly. "I didn't mean to come on so strong, kid. It's the same game we're in, no matter which side you're on. I honed my talents in the Justice Department myself. I reckon that seventy-five percent of the defense lawyers in this country were prosecutors in their misspent youth. I've read you, and you have a first-rate mind. Any time you want to switch teams and come work for me in Miami, I'll take you on just like that."

"My husband too?" Meg returned, astonishing herself by responding half-seriously to the offer.

"Why not? Can't split up the Dauntless Duncans. Not that I wouldn't try if you gave me the slightest bit of encouragement. I was always a fool for a perfect chin." He winked broadly, then focused his blue-gray eyes on the vista offered by the small rectangular window to his right.

Meg leaned back in her seat, a sigh of exasperation escaping her lips. Here was one of the fine minds of her time—reduced to the banalities of the airborne come-on.

Now, if her associate Andrea Roberts were sitting here, she'd flirt right back, giving as good as she got—though she was as single-mindedly in love with her Ed as Meg was with Don. Louisiana-born Andrea always said the trouble with Meg was that she'd grown up in Boston, and therefore didn't know the difference between flirtation and seduction.

Maybe so, Meg had to concede. Or maybe it was just that her

combination of innocent, determined face, lean limbs, and flamboyant breasts somehow invited more than her share of male attention. Andrea had the dark, wavy hair and alabaster skin of the classic southern belle, but she had a matronly softness—covering a sharp legal mind—that seemed to take her out of the sex-object category.

The Cessna began its descent, and Meg peered across Victor Green and out the window. Flying at night provided a magnificent spectacle, especially when you were in a small aircraft, low enough to see the twinkling lights of civilization. Meg wasn't blind to the beauty of sky and water and flower and bird, but man-made beauty always enticed and reassured her in a way that natural wonders didn't.

She stole another glance at the picture of her and Don. He shared her enthusiasm for the created rather than the natural. God, if only he were there. The closer she got to Key West, the more fearful she grew about Win's condition. The situation would be so much easier to handle if she knew that she would be lying in the comforting circle of her husband's arms before the night was over. She just hoped that the Washington weather lifted with the dawn and Don got off the ground first thing.

"You're sure you're not a nervous flier?" Green asked, picking up her tension. "I'd be happy to hold your hand for the touchdown."

"I'm fine, thanks," Meg said stiffly.

"If this is fine, kid, I'd hate to see you when you're upset. Don't forget my job offer," he added, as the wheels of the plane crunched down on the runway. "Miami's a helluva lot nicer than Washington in the winter. In the summer, too, as far as that goes. I'd find you and Don a nice little house in Coconut Grove with a swimming pool and tennis court. I bet you're a killer on the court. And keep in mind that it's a lot more soul-satisfying to protect the rights of people fleeing oppressive regimes than it is to get them deported."

"Dammit," Meg returned angrily, "I'm in the business of protecting people just as much as you are. I protect the jobs of native-born Americans who are struggling as it is in this economy. As far as I'm concerned, you're not doing anyone a favor by encouraging illegal immigration. You've been in migrant workers' camps, haven't you? No one should have to live like that."

"I couldn't agree with you more," Victor Green said quietly, unbuckling his seat belt. "I told you we were ultimately fighting the same battle."

His words rang in her ears as she endured a rickety taxi ride out to the marina where the *Agualinda* was moored. Then, as she stood on the lonely dock with her bags at her feet, a vast echoing emptiness pushed all words from her mind.

The landscape was the perfect visual counterpart to her state of mind. Black skies and black sea rushed to meet each other, the sliver of a moon and the thick sprinkling of stars offering points of brightness but no real light. Though she could hear a faint hum of humanity from the Half Shell, a quarter of a mile toward town, there was precious little else in the way of civilized presence. Of the six houseboats moored at the dock, only the *Agualinda* showed signs of being inhabited. Crickets were making a din, giving Meg an eerie reminder that she and her kind were vastly outnumbered on earth.

She loved the turn-of-the-century New England-style dwellings—the "Conch" houses—of Key West's Old Town; and she could appreciate, if not love, the island's semitropical vegetation. But the scene she was part of right now was just plain desolate by even the most romantic standards.

Shivering, she picked up her bags and started to make her way along the dock. Her pace was slow because she was as afraid of what she would find on the *Agualinda* as she was reluctant to remain alone in the uninviting night.

The thought of Win in pain, possibly dying, was hardly endurable. She wanted him to last forever—though he was already seventy-nine, and "forever" was rapidly getting closer.

Meg had been only fifteen when her parents were killed in a train accident. Win and his then-wife, Carlotta, had brought her up in their Beacon Hill house. Though Carlotta had been kind, Meg's real bond had always been with the opinionated, robust, emotional Win rather than his wispy, humorless wife. Neither Meg nor Win had been overwhelmed by loss when Carlotta withdrew from the household, taking most of the family silver with her. Meg went to college and law school in Boston so as not to abandon her uncle, but when the Justice Department beckoned, Win urged her to answer the summons and move to Washington. He'd remained in the Beacon Hill house long enough to provide a gorgeous setting for Meg and Don's wedding. Then, partly out of curiosity, partly to keep Meg from clucking over him, he'd taken one long trip after another. Refusing the Duncans' repeated invitations to live with them in Georgetown, he'd finally settled in Key West. Meg never had stopped clucking, but she couldn't deny that his strange life afloat seemed to agree with him.

But now she couldn't help wondering if his bohemian existence had finally done him in. Had she and Don been negligent, fooling themselves about Win's self-sufficiency?

"You come down here to bay at the moon or to visit me?" a familiar voice called out from the *Agualinda*, tearing Meg's heart with its tremulous quality. Win had always infused his Beacon Hill broad *a*'s with a barroom resonance.

"Win!" she shouted gaily, hurrying toward him, her city sandals clattering on the worn wooden dock.

"Don't break your neck on me, old girl," her uncle cautioned. "This is supposed to be my deathbed, not yours."

"Deathbed, my eye," she chided, stepping aboard the *Agualinda* and throwing her arms around her uncle. Feeling his frailness, she had to force back tears. "Fact is," she said, with a pause to bestow kisses, "I wouldn't have torn down here in such a hurry if I'd known you were ambulatory—you faker, you."

"You mean you were looking forward to emptying my bedpan?" Laughing at his own words, Win suddenly doubled up in a coughing fit and sank, shuddering, onto a piece of furniture that was utterly unnautical but utterly Win—a Boston rocker. Meg huddled over him, stroking back the wispy white hair. Until this moment he had always impressed her as being a vibrantly striking if unconventional figure, with his mariner's whites and a captain's hat set rakishly on his head. Now, sitting there in his eternal Brooks Brothers' blue-and-white striped seersucker robe, he seemed to be someone whose life had shifted into the past tense. The vital force was simply gone.

"What may I get you to drink?" Win asked, as soon as he had breath to speak.

Meg felt as though she'd been hurled back into her childhood by that question. Her mother had always told her that good Boston manners dictated the phrasing, "What may I get you to drink?" The alternative "Would you like a drink?" was considered too tentative an offer of hospitality. Win would always remain a gentleman—wherever he was, however he was.

"Club soda would be nice, and I remember where it is," she said, starting up the steps that led to the kitchen alcove. "What would you like, Unc?"

"Nothing that's in your power to give me, girl," Win said after her. "I'm dying, and don't let's insult each other by pretending I'm not."

Stifling a moan, supporting herself against the sink, Meg fought the impulse to rush back to her uncle's rocker. But clearly he'd chosen to make his announcement while she was out of sight—as though the few yards' separation could ease the terrible moment.

"Don't let's pretend it's a tragedy either," Win went on, his voice even. "I've gotten to do everything I've wanted in this life except see your children, and I guess I could outlive Methuselah and not manage that. I'm leaving it all to you and Don," he went on, as Meg blindly opened the refrigerator door and groped for a bottle of club soda. "Except for one of the floating homes, which I'm leaving to Flip at the Half Shell."

Meg began pouring club soda with an unsteady hand as Win's words sank in. "But Unc—"

"Let me finish, darlin'," he interrupted gently. "Now, enough of your lawyer's brain has rubbed off on me so I know there's no such thing as a conditional will. But I'm kind of hoping you'll sell the house in Beacon Hill and live on the *Agualinda* instead of the other way around. You'll get your sea legs, girl."

Trusting herself not to burst into the tears Win obviously dreaded seeing, Meg started back down the stairs toward him, forcing her lips to hint at a smile.

"You know I get sick every time I so much as look at a boat," she said, as if that were the main issue at stake.

Win waved away her objection. "The plain fact is, the *Agualinda* isn't a boat. It may have a hull, but it doesn't have an engine, does it? It's one big waterbed, is what it is."

Meg pulled up a needlepointed ottoman and perched on it, taking a long draught from her glass and staring soberly at her uncle.

"But, darling Unc," she said, forcing her voice to stay steady, "Don and I are committed to Washington. We can't live in either Boston or Key West."

"Tush, girl, you can live anywhere you want. Through no virtue of my own, I'm a very rich man. The two of you will have a hundred thousand a year without going into capital. And that's after the damned government has taken its tax bite. If you want to keep the Beacon Hill house for the rental income, you can do that, or you can sell the old monstrosity and go play tennis in the south of France for a year. You can do anything, beginning with telling the Justice Department to gazump itself."

Despite the underlying gloom of the moment, Meg burst out laughing. Though she admired the Attorney General and the man she reported to directly, there *was* something oppressive about the idea of a boss, any boss. She didn't seek power over other people, but she didn't like the idea of anyone having power over her. It would be rather fabulous to say, smiling, "Go gazump yourself."

"Win," she said to her uncle, "I promise that when the time comes, Don and I will use the money in a manner that honors your spirit. But we're not in any hurry, and I won't have you rushing us. You've got to let me call in a doctor. Pneumonia may have been fatal when you were a boy, but it's no big deal now. There's no reason to give up." She folded her arms across her chest. "I thought you were the one who taught me to fight, fight, fight."

A spasm of coughing shook Win. When it had passed, the frail white-haired man said, "I don't have pneumonia, and you know it. What I've got they can't cure with antibiotics. I've lived the way I've wanted to live, and I'll die the way I want to die, and if you can't take it, girl, you get back to Miami or Washington or wherever you want."

"Are you in pain?" Meg asked softly.

Win shook his head. "I've got pills, girl. Powerful pills. I don't believe in suffering. And I'm not selfish enough to let you see me in pain. What time is Don getting here?"

"About noon, the skies permitting."

"Let's have a dinner party tomorrow night. The three of us and Flip. You learn how to cook yet?"

"Nope. I've just gotten handier with a credit card."

"Then we'll order in from the Half Shell and Cap'n Bob's. Conch fritters, and spiny lobster, and we ought to have avocados, and key lime pie for dessert. You like whipped cream or meringue on your key lime pie?"

"You're testing me after all these years together?" Meg returned. "Whipped cream, of course. Don, too."

"I knew I could count on the two of you."

To Meg's astonishment, she was beginning to feel a strange kind of merriment building within her. But why not? A remarkable human being was sitting in front of her, and she loved him, and he loved her, and that was what counted most. Half the grief at deathbeds, she suspected, was grief over a life not lived to the full or love never given expression until it was too late. There would be no place for that kind of grief on the *Agualinda*.

"I think this dinner party calls for champagne," she said. "Think I can scout up some Dom Perignon tomorrow?"

"Now you're in the spirit of things," Win said, reaching for her hand. "What do you say to a game of cribbage?"

# Chapter 3

THE FOURTH OF JULY HAD COME AND GONE A WEEK AGO, but the scene in front of Meg and Don might have been painted to honor that day. The vast sky and the waters of the Gulf of Mexico rivaled each other in the brilliance of their blues. The *Agualinda*, freshly painted, and the whipped-cream clouds in the sky were a guileless white. Half a dozen blooms in the wooden flowerbox under the single front window of the floating house provided a piercing note of red.

The Duncans twined their arms around each other's waists, taking in the colors and shapes before them, not quite daring to talk, not quite wanting to move to the oaken door.

*Their* door, Meg realized. Their very own front door. Their own home: the cozy cottage they'd never remotely dreamed of having and still weren't sure they wanted. At least, *she* wasn't sure. Don had been in a kind of ecstatic dither ever since they'd made the decision to come live in Key West.

"Why do I want to carry you across the threshold?" he asked now.

"It must be the geraniums in the windowbox," Meg said, looking at the scarlet flowers nodding their heads in the gentle sea breeze. "They make me feel as though I'm supposed to plunk on an

23

apron as soon as we get inside and make you some chocolate chip cookies."

Her tone of voice was so glum that both of them laughed.

"Only you can make baking sound slightly more despicable than robbing little old ladies," Don said. "Those aren't ordinary geraniums, by the way. They're *Ixora fulgens*."

"You're putting me on," Meg protested.

"Nope," Don said proudly. "Also known as flame of the woods or jungle geraniums. The twigs supposedly can cure toothaches."

Meg couldn't hold back a feeling of betrayal. "Since when did you become such a nature boy? You're the fellow who told me the reason he always sent me roses on my birthday was that he didn't know the name of any other flower."

"Did I say that?" Don pushed back the shock of straight brown hair that forever threatened his forehead. "I suppose I did. Ed Roberts gave me a field guide to subtropical plants. I kind of got into it. I brought it with me, if you're interested." He gestured toward the enormous heap of duffel bags at their feet. "I should be able to locate it in a week or two."

"No thanks," Meg said stiffly, not knowing why she was carrying on but unable to stop herself. "I wonder who put the flowers there," she said in an effort at civility. "Flip, I suppose."

Don gave her a little hug. "Darling, we're going to be happy. I know we are. We made the right decision."

"Did we truly?" Meg blurted out. Her stomach was churning, whether because of the slight motion of the dock or because of anxiety she wasn't quite sure. "Or did we just come here because we knew Win wanted us to?" Her voice caught as she uttered her uncle's name. She had honored his wish that she refrain from "crepe hanging," but eight months after his death she still had trouble believing he wasn't somehow going to pop up. He had always been so *there*. She stared at the door of the *Agualinda*, willing it to open from within. Then, shaking her head at her own foolishness, she hoisted a duffel bag and said, "Let's go in."

"You're not cheating me of my moment." Don took the bag from her hand and set it down with a thump. He scooped her up in his arms, dropping kisses into her hair. "Here we go," he said, carrying her up the span of carpeted gangplank that led from the dock to the *Agualinda*. He cradled her with his left arm as his right hand fumbled the key into the lock. He pushed open the door. "Be it ever so damp, there's no place like home."

Meg inhaled a lungful of mildew, disinfectant, fresh paint, brine, and just plain moisture—and promptly burst into tears. Don carried her over to the built-in canvas-covered loveseat that served as the living room's principal piece of furniture, and sat down next to her, holding her close.

"I'd say those tears were overdue," he commented tenderly. He found a large white handkerchief in his pocket and offered it. "Win was a fabulous man, darling. I miss him, too."

"Oh, Don," Meg sobbed, "I'm not just crying for Uncle Win, and it's no good pretending I am. I'm plain scared. Is this really the life for us? I know, I know," she added, as he began to interrupt. "We thrashed it all out back in Washington, and it's no good going through the old arguments. I made up my mind, and I made it up freely, but I can't for the life of me remember why!" Her voice rose to a wail, and she buried her face in her husband's polo-shirted chest.

He silently stroked her until the shaking and sobbing stopped. Then he kissed her forehead, her cheeks, and her famous chin—which was quivering now, not tilting northward at its usual challenging angle. He made murmuring sounds of reassurance.

"We haven't done anything irrevocable," he said when she lay against him, her tears all spent. "If we don't like our new life, we can always go back to the old one. Maybe not get exactly the same apartment and jobs, but something so near alike you'll hardly know the difference. We're off on an adventure, not a prison term." Cupping her chin and raising her face so her eyes met his, he added, "We've brought the most important element from our old life with us, anyway—ourselves. Our love for each other. The marriage. Listen, with a great romance, a built-in tennis partner, and a cool hundred grand a year, how bad can life be?"

Meg smiled at him and reached out to touch his face with her strong fingers. He was truly her reference to all reality. She knew the day was hot because, sliding her fingers down his neck, she could feel his sweat. She knew she was still anxious because the pounding of his heart told her what he saw revealed in her eyes.

Dear Win had always claimed she loved anxiety, that she and Don thrived on it. Maybe part of what she was anxious about was that here, in Key West, she would no longer have anything to be anxious about! She burst into laughter.

"Share the joke," Don commanded gently. She shared it, and his laughter joined hers. "Are you afraid it's only a matter of days before you think the most important thing on earth is collecting shells?"

"Something like that," Meg admitted.

"Don't worry," Don said. "There's that newsstand on Duval that carries *The New York Times* and the Washington *Post*. Shall we drive right up there so you can get a fix? Read all the dire headlines and keep your adrenal glands going? Come on. We'll just stick the bags inside in case it rains and then we can, tootle into town." He eyed her suggestively. "Unless you'd like to exercise some other glands . . ."

Meg put both her hands flat against his chest. "I could be persuaded. Especially if you turn on the air conditioner."

Don reached over and turned a dial. He looked at his watch, waggling his thick auburn eyebrows. "Do you realize that at this hour all God-fearing lawyers are settling down for the afternoon grind, as their stomachs turn lunch into acid indigestion? The big question on their minds is how they're going to get all their work done: Should they cancel their dinner plans for this evening or come into the office tomorrow at dawn—or maybe do both?" He brought his lips tenderly down on Meg's. "I think I'd slightly rather make love with you, darling. Have we done it on a Wednesday afternoon since our honeymoon, do you think?"

Putting their arms around each other, they kissed again. Out of the corner of her eye, Meg glimpsed the cobalt waters of the Gulf through the wide window behind the loveseat. The sea was bobbing up and down, or maybe it was the *Agualinda* that was moving. Meg screwed her eyes shut as nausea threatened, concentrating with all her might on Don's ardent mouth. His tongue lapped tenderly at the borders of her lips, then heatedly tried to force her lips apart. She denied him admission for the pure pleasure of feeling him persist. Moaning, she finally yielded, allowing him the liberty of her mouth. As she tasted his juices, her own tongue became a wild explorer.

"Don, my love. Don."

"Yes, darling. I know. Me, too. I want you, Meg." His hands went to her breasts, lingered for an electrifying moment, then slid down to her thighs. "These sure beat office clothes," he said, as his hands disappeared underneath her wide denim skirt and flirted with her stocking-less thighs. His fingers teased at the lacy edges of her bikini panties. "But I think you should go all the way and wear skimpy shorts and halter tops. I've spent too many lonely days and nights apart from you over the past ten years. I want instant access from now on."

As he withdrew his hands to work on the buttons at her waist, Meg felt a sudden lurching inside her stomach that had nothing to do with sex.

"Don," she groaned, "I think I'm going to be sick." Hand clapped to her mouth, she ran up three stairs and through the kitchen to the tiny green-tiled bathroom. Standing there retching miserably, she decided that the color of the bathroom had been all too aptly chosen. Afterward, she splashed cold water on her face and thought longingly of the toothbrush, paste, and licorice mouthwash out on the deck in one of her suitcases.

"Darling?" Don called solicitously.

"I'll live," Meg managed to say. "But I'm not sure I *want* to. That's what my mother used to say about seasickness when I was a little girl—you never died of it, you just wished you would."

"You're sure it's seasickness and not my sexual technique?" Don opened the door to the bathroom and handed her a large plaid plastic case. "I thought you might want the old toilet kit."

"Bless you." Meg freshened up and then, with a resigned sigh, began putting makeup, deodorant, shampoos, and an assortment of basic remedies into the medicine chest. Endowed with robust health, and somewhat sharing her late uncle's skepticism about the health industry, Meg had never believed much in pills and potions. Don had teased her that her lack of interest in filling the refrigerator was exceeded only by her lack of interest in filling the medicine chest. But before leaving Washington for the Keys, Meg had raided the local discount drugstore, as if she were leaving the last civilized outpost and heading for the barbarian depths.

Now she contemplated her bottle of Dramamine. For the moment her stomach felt steady—empty, but steady. If she took Dramamine, she'd get sleepy. If she didn't take Dramamine, and looked out the big window again, she might tumble back into that spinning agony.

Don came up behind her, putting gentle hands on her shoulders. "Playing drugstore? I was hoping you might be restored enough to get back to what we started."

Guiltily Meg realized that the sexual moment had passed for her. "I'd rather wait until I'm sure I won't have to leap up in the middle again." She smiled at Don's reflection in the mirror. "Am I the funnest date you ever had?"

"By leaps and bounds, my pretty: I always knew if I got you off the mainland, life would be one long bed romp." He moved his hands down the slopes of her breasts, tweaking her nipples with a teasing familiarity, then giving her a gentle pat on the bottom. "This may sound like a ghastly idea, but we should probably go get something to eat. The prevailing wisdom on seasickness is that you shouldn't let your stomach be totally empty. True?"

"True, counselor. Why don't we go up to the Half Shell? I don't know if I can face conch fritters yet, but we ought to let Flip know we're here. *You* can eat fritters, you rat, and I'll nibble on a saltine." They piled their belongings in the small living room, then looked around for a silent minute.

"It's really very cute," Don said finally.

Meg took in the bright solid colors of the pillows heaped on the loveseat, the pale lacquered knotty pine paneling, the old Boston rocker Win had loved, the oval hooked rug barely visible beneath the duffel bags. For the moment the water seemed to be holding its breath, and she took advantage of the absence of motion to study the vast sweep of blue that was their backyard. A flight of wooden steps carried her eye "upstairs" to a large sleeping loft and dressing area, with the same panoramic view of sky and sea.

It *was* cute. But since when had she or Don liked cuteness? Their

Georgetown apartment had been notable for its clean lines, sophisticated spare furniture, and cool minimalist paintings. Neither plant nor pet had interfered with the man-made orderliness. The couple to whom they'd sublet the apartment, paintings and all, had praised the way the "space" left them alone.

Now Meg said doubtfully, "Didn't you like the way we lived before?"

"Of course I did," Don said, jumping over a bag to put his arms around her. "But that doesn't mean it was the only good life in the universe. The only good life for us." He rocked her gently, stroking her straight brown hair, then pushed some behind an ear and nibbled on the lobe.

Meg stared at the international collection of beer mugs, thirty or forty pints and halfpints in glass and ceramic, hanging on the wall behind the rocker. "I love this stuff for being Win's, but without him here . . ." Her voice trailed off, and she shook her head. "I wish we'd brought one painting," she said lamely. "At least some of the computer graphics. We could just fit a pair of Cahn's conformal mappings where the beer mugs are."

"Then you'd worry about the dampness getting to them," Don said. "Remember how we used to get a kick out of being separated because it was so much fun getting together again? Until we'd done it once too often? Well, it will be fun seeing our art again someday."

"Someday," Meg repeated softly. They'd sublet their apartment for a year. Don had said again and again that they didn't have to stay on the *Agualinda* for a year, that they didn't have to stay on it for one minute longer than they wanted to. They had lots and lots of money, lots and lots of choices. But she knew he felt challenged by the dramatic change in their way of life. She sensed that he would feel a failure if they turned around in less than a year.

Her stomach clenched again—this time from emotion, not the sea. Don's excitement over the change unsettled her a bit. Hadn't he loved their old life as much as she had? Had he sometimes peered out their shared windows with a secretly restless heart? Another part of her mind told her not to be a fool. Wasn't the core of his desire for change a desire to have more time with her? A wife could hardly feel threatened by such a wish.

In any event, she'd agreed to the change—months ago, when Win's will was probated. Never mind that she now questioned her wisdom in making that agreement. Maybe she'd said yes partly to please Don and partly to honor Win's memory, but she'd also been answering needs of her own. The nights away from Don *had* become torturous. Her work *had* become stale. The bottom line was that she'd embarked on this mad adventure freely, and there was no point standing there sulking. Don would have every right to be disappointed in such behavior—to be furious, in fact.

She loosed a small storm of kisses over Don's face, lingering on a patch of beard his razor had missed that morning. "I love you, Donald Duncan, Esquire," she said. "And you, too, Don Duncan, ex-lawyer and human-being-at-large. And—and—let's go upstairs," she begged, suddenly sizzling with desire as his scent filled her nostrils. "The Half Shell will have to wait. You can have Venus on the half shell first."

"Convince me," Don said, a smile playing at the corner of his mouth, giving his easygoing, boyish face an appealing devilish air.

Meg thrust her hands under his striped polo shirt. Her fingers wandered, softly through the warm mat of hair, then grew urgent, her fingernails lightly grazing his skin. As Don groaned with pleasure, she lifted his shirt and put her mouth where her fingers had been. Her teeth nipped; her tongue soothed. Her lips closed around each flat, hard nipple, then raced in spirals over his chest, as if her mouth were a brush and his chest a canvas.

"Meg, darling. Meg." Don's hands made wild motions in her hair. "You don't know how fantastic that feels."

"Oh, I might have some idea. Well, have I convinced you? You gonna take me upstairs, big boy?"

"I'll take you anywhere you want," Don said. "On top of the luggage. Anywhere."

"I'd like to do it on the loveseat, and in the shower, and maybe against the kitchen sink—but for now I feel like a bed." Meg started up the wooden steps. "Oh, Don. Look."

The queen-size Japanese futon had been unrolled and freshly made up with crisp blue linens. A wine carafe filled with yellow, red, and apricot roses stood between the futon and the enormous window, brilliant in the vast light, sweetening the air.

"How darling of Flip," Meg said.

Don cleared his throat and gave a smile of patently false innocence.

"How darling of you?" Meg said.

Don nodded. "Flip did the doing, but it was my idea," Don said. "You see? I may know all about *Ixora fulgens*, but I'm never going to stop sending you roses."

"You—" Meg began, only to be hurled, shrieking, into Don's arms as the houseboat lurched violently. Tumbling onto the futon, they heard the unmistakable roar and whoosh of a speedboat. Meg looked out the window and saw a sleek silver blur go whizzing by, so close to the *Agualinda* that she automatically recoiled.

"The three o'clock bus to Key Largo," Don joked, but Meg heard a tremor in his voice.

She stretched out on the futon, face up, hands pressed to her belly, taking deep breaths. She willed her stomach to calm, the houseboat to calm, the world to calm.

"You okay?" Don knelt next to her, tenderly pushing her hair back off her damp forehead.

"Sorry to be such a baby," she said, smiling weakly.

"Listen, darling, that scared me plenty, too. I wonder if that's a regular occurrence. Are you still nauseated?"

"I'm fine. Almost fine. Make love to me, Don. I need you. Bring me back to reality—the reality of us."

Wordlessly he freed her from the burden of clothes, and then, his admiring eyes on the swells and valleys of her body, he undressed himself. He reached across the roses to let down a wide bamboo shade.

"In case anyone on the east coast of Mexico is looking out the window," he said.

Meg sighed contentedly at the aura of intimacy created by the filtered light. She pulled Don's hands to her breasts, making throaty noises as her nipples burst into bloom at his touch.

With his fingers, then his tongue, he traced the line of demarcation between the cream of her breasts and the coffee of the tanned skin above. "Vanilla and chocolate," he murmured. "And strawberry," he added, closing his lips around each nipple in turn. "You are the world's most delicious woman."

"Even seasick and moody?"

"Even," Don said. "Isn't that what we vowed? Loyalty even unto greenness about the gills and vile crabbiness?"

"I didn't think I'd been vilely crabby," Meg said, shifting slightly away from Don's touch.

"And I didn't say you had been. Just that I'd love you even-if you were. I must say, my darling Meg, that you do seem to be doing your best to *get* yourself crabby."

Meg sat up, hugging her knees. "Do you have the feeling we're destined not to make love right now?"

Don tousled her hair. "You New England puritan, you. You just don't feel right doing it on a weekday afternoon."

"It's not all *my* fault," Meg flared. "I didn't ask that damned speedboat to come hurtling by." Then, appalled at her own tone of voice, she said contritely, "Oh, Don, I'm sorry. I'm sorry. I'm being impossible. I'll get over it, I promise. Let's go to the Half Shell and gorge on conch fritters. Key lime pie, too. If I'm going to throw up later, I don't have to worry about calories, right?"

Don laughed. "Now that sounds like the woman I've spent the last ten years with. Thank God we didn't leave her back in Washington. The Half Shell it is. Last one dressed buys the beer."

Meg scrambled into her clothes, pausing only to press her lips to Don's. But the kiss tasted wrong. The air still felt tense and her stomach was still asking questions.

She pulled up the bamboo blind and covertly eyed Don as he bent to tie the laces on his sneakers. For a weird, unsettling moment she realized she was seeing his face from a brand-new angle, seeing him in a way she had never before glimpsed him in ten years of marriage. Panic rose in her throat. Don turned his head a fraction of an inch, making himself familiar again. Yet all the way up to the Half Shell a notion persisted in Meg's mind. In this strange new life her husband himself could seem a stranger.

She didn't like the idea at all.

# Chapter 4

Locking the front door of the *Agualinda*, Don said, "You've got to admit that we have the prettiest house on the block."

"Some block," Meg said with bite. As she stood in the late afternoon sun surveying the five floating homes her uncle had bequeathed them, and the one he'd left to Flip Peterson, she thought she'd never in all her life seen such an architectural jumble.

At one end was the *Agualinda*, with its relentlessly cheery Cape Cod air. At the other end was Flip's *Flying Onion*, with a mosquelike dome and cupola grandly ornamenting the roof. The four unoccupied houseboats bobbing in between were most nearly classifiable as Mock Tudor, Southern Plantation (complete with columns), Ye Old Weathered Shingles, and Stark Modern.

Don gave Meg a little shake. "Are you the Meg Duncan who used to kick and scream every time we drove through one of those New England towns where all the houses on Main Street matched perfectly? I seem to remember you muttering 'Unconstitutional!' when you learned there were town ordinances requiring everyone to paint white, have black shutters, and wear red Shetland sweaters."

Meg had to laugh at his exaggeration. She reached up to clasp the hand he'd left lying on her shoulder.

"You never let me get away with anything." She sighed. "Can't I be inconsistent every year or so? Its—what's today—the eleventh? We'll name July eleventh National Inconsistency Day."

"Sorry," Don said firmly. "It's the unwritten part of our marriage contract that we make each other toe the line. Besides, today's the twelfth."

Again Meg felt a flutter of panic. How could she not know what day it was? Meg Duncan was someone who knew the day and the time and what the President had said at his last press conference and who was on the Davis Cup team. Swaying slightly, she steadied herself against Don, unsure whether the dock was moving or her legs were echoing her undulating mind.

Tightening his hold on her, Don scattered kisses over her head.

"Your hair tastes so warm and salty and good," he said.

"Like clam broth? How sexy."

"Clam broth *is* sexy," Don insisted, undaunted by her sardonic tone. "Compared to cream of celery soup, say." His hand slid down to her waist. Steering her along the dock toward the road, he added, "I'm not going to let you be unhappy here, you know. I'm not going to let us be unhappy."

"Has someone appointed you admiral?" Meg asked stiffly.

"Are you forgetting everything about the way we operate, darling? Just because we've made a change in our geography doesn't mean we've changed the ground rules. Moods are as contagious down here as they are in Washington, and if I refuse to catch your bad mood, you're just going to have to catch my good mood. The defense rests. Look at that, will you?" His finger traced the flight of a pure silvery-white streak of feathers across the cobalt skies.

"I suppose you're going to start learning bird names, too," Meg said. "To go with your *Angora fulgens.*"

"*Ixora fulgens.*" Don corrected her, just a trace of sharpness in his voice. Then he added, with deliberate lightness, "I promise to confine myself to identifying man-made objects. Look at that telephone pole up there. A perfect specimen. And there goes an automobile, subspecies Porsche," he said, as a bright red ovoid whizzed by them, leaving the proverbial cloud of dust behind.

Meg stared after the sleek convertible. A flash of blond hair from the jump seat rang a loud bell.

"I think I know whose car that is," she exclaimed. "Do you remember my telling you about the kid I saved from drowning at the Coconut Grove Hotel last December? Before Win . . . when Win . . ." She swallowed, unable to complete the sentence.

"Sure, I remember." Putting a comforting arm around her waist, Don added, "But how could you recognize anyone in that car? They must have been going seventy-five."

"Well, you could see it was a little girl—and without a kiddie seat or even a seat belt, judging from the way she was moving around. Just what I'd expect from those parents. Life in the fast lane, without seat belts. And her hair was pretty memorable. That really yellow blond."

As they moved up the road toward the Half Shell, Don said, "I don't ever remember a kid making such an impression on you before. She must have been quite a character."

"Yeah—a first-class brat. You're right, I probably just imagined that I recognized her. Stupid."

They walked along in silence. Meg fixed her eyes on the low sheds and shacks at the water's edge, at the big blueness beyond. Forcing herself to take deep breaths of the tangy sea air, she tried to find pleasure in the rough honesty of the vista and the clarity of the afternoon. She watched a shrimp trawler mooring, its exuberant young crew looping thick ropes around the weathered posts that lined the dock like so many sentinels. But she couldn't lose herself in the bustle around her. Her own strange mood kept getting in the way.

Whatever must Don be thinking? She let her senses focus on the warmth and heft of the arm he had around her, on the lime in his after-shave lotion. After ten years together, they knew one another by heart—and part of the knowing was a recognition of the stranger in the other. She wanted to reassure him that her stranger wasn't taking over, that she was just in a troubled mood. Only first she had to reassure herself. She couldn't shake off the frightening feeling that Don's old Meg, the real Meg, the never-down-for-long Meg, had been left back in Washington.

She felt certain of only one thing at the moment: The move to Key West had been a gargantuan miscalculation. She'd honored her uncle's wishes, but she'd paid too high a price. She'd betrayed her own nature—the last thing Win would have wanted. And Don meanwhile had the bouncy walk and starry-eyed gaze of a man reborn! Oh, God, how were they going to reconcile their different mindsets? Easier, far easier, to resolve an argument. There wasn't any right or wrong here— just a gap as wide as the Gulf of Mexico!

"Calliope," Don said suddenly.

"What?"

"That was the kid's name, wasn't it?"

"I guess so," Meg said, somehow not wanting to admit that she remembered the child's name perfectly well. "Something outrageous like that."

"We'd probably name one after some point of law," Don said. "Res Ipsa Loquitur Duncan." He pulled Meg over as a family of four on mopeds went varooming unsteadily by. Meg stared wonderingly at the scantily dressed group, the epitome of carefree vacationers with their grins and shouts.

"Meg? Are you ever sorry? That we decided not to have kids?" Don asked.

"Am I ever sorry?" Meg stammered. She could scarcely believe the question. When Don had asked her to marry him, she'd told him—as if it were a shameful secret she had to confess—that she didn't want to have children. To her vast relief, Don had said he agreed with her. They'd made it a point to avoid the issue ever since. Most of their close friends, like Ed and Andrea Roberts, were people who had also chosen to remain "childfree."

Now Don commented, "It's just that I remember your saying you didn't want to reproduce because you didn't see the point of having kids, then turning them over to strangers to raise while you went about being a lawyer. Or having kids and staying home with them and letting your education go to waste."

"And you agreed!" Meg said heatedly.

"Of course I agreed." Laughter edged Don's voice. "My God, you're touchy today, darling. Or am I just somehow managing to say all the wrong things?"

"There are no wrong things to say between us," Meg mumbled. She kicked a pebble and watched it skitter down the dusty road. "What are you getting at?"

"Just that our life has changed. We no longer go off at eight o'clock every morning and return God knows when."

"And therefore we should immediately have four kids," Meg said, her voice rising. "Each one could have its own houseboat, right? They're about the size of kids' playhouses. And with all that rocking motion, we could save the expense of cradles. Why didn't I think of it myself?"

"Meg, I didn't mean—"

"Oh, Don," she cried, clutching his arm, "have you wanted children all along? Did you secretly hope we'd defeat the IUD? Have you thought of me as an unnatural woman because I don't have the usual maternal fantasies? Tell me the truth," she pleaded, stopping in her tracks and pulling him around to face her. She searched the brown-gold pools of his eyes. "Is that how you've felt?"

"Meg. Meg." He Crushed her to his chest. "Here's how I've felt for the last ten years. I've thought of myself as the luckiest man on earth. There were days when I could hardly believe the world had been so good to me—giving me you, and good health, and work I cared about, and our wonderful friends, and our home. For ten years I wanted only one thing: for us to go on forever, exactly the way we were."

"Truly?" Meg murmured into the stripes of his shirt.

"Truly," came the tender response. "I even had a vision of us dying together—at age ninety-six, on a tennis court, after winning our match against some upstart octogenarians. But when Win left us, and we began to make changes, all sorts of doors started flying open in my mind. *You* were the one who opened the door marked 'children'—back in December, when you told me about saving Calliope from drowning. There was something in your voice that made me wonder if *you* hadn't secretly wanted children all along—and had suppressed the desire because you knew I didn't have the usual paternal inclinations." Drawing breath, he added, "So you've got it all backward, you see."

"Well, let's not end up with you thinking we've got to have a child for my sake, and me thinking we've got to have one for your sake," Meg said lightly, her heartbeat returning to something like normal.

"No, let's not do that," Don agreed as they threaded their way among the cars, vans, motorcycles, and mopeds parked in front of the Half Shell.

Flip Peterson leaped across the bar to greet them, calling out an order for conch fritters before Meg and Don so much as said hello.

"You got a pearl earring," Meg exclaimed, hugging the ponytailed young bartender. "I don't believe you. Are you trying out for the Guinness Book of Records?"

Flip unself-consciously fingered an earlobe that sported a tiny diamond stud, a silver cross, and five different miniature gold ornaments, as well as the new pearl.

"You know we don't go in for understatement in Key West. I found it in an oyster here this winter. Couldn't pass that up, could I? Hey, it's great to see you guys. The *Agualinda* look okay?" he asked, going back to the working side of the bar and opening two bottles of Rolling Rock.

"It looks beautiful," Meg said. "The flowers, and the paint, and the fresh sheets—" She stopped, blushing, but she was too late.

Flip roared with laughter, slapping one of the thighs left bare by his cutoff jeans.

"Tried out the futon right away, did you? That's the Key West spirit, all right."

He moved off to get beer for a gaggle of leather-jacketed bikers crowded together along one side of the spacious bar. Looking at the good-natured gang as she sipped her own beer, then turning to watch an old-fashioned wooden fan make lazy circles above her, Meg had to concede that Key West did have a unique spirit. She knew, too, that despite her uneasiness of the past several hours, the place still held enormous charm.

The Key West ethic was simple. Anything went—as long as no one got hurt. If people had an obligation to each other, it was to be as amusing as possible. Freedom was the island goddess. "Enjoy!" was the regional anthem.

Meg had found Boston and Washington challenging rather than restrictive, but some secret bohemian spark in her soul always ignited in Key West. Though she didn't want to wear black leather or puncture her earlobes—and though she could never have tolerated the uncertainties of the hand-to-mouth existence of some of the Key West street people—she was glad to be among such larky spirits.

She smiled fondly at Don, who was tracing a heart in the frost of his beer mug. She had to admire his ability to make the leap from their old life to the new with such apparent ease and grace. He hadn't really changed, she reassured herself. She was just seeing the flip side of the usual coin. He worked intensely, he played tennis intensely, he made love intensely—and now he was relaxing intensely.

Rubbing his back, she felt a faint dampness beneath his shirt. She was suddenly overcome by a longing to taste his mouth, his sweat, all his juices. Air conditioners had their place, but there was a lot to be said for the utter physicality of making love in the tropical summer heat. She swayed on her bar stool, thinking ahead to the sultry encounter awaiting them.

She wanted him so much that she didn't want him right away; this longing deserved to be savored.

"Let's go be tourists," she murmured. "Hemingway House, and the southernmost point, and then Mallory Square for the sunset, and maybe a drink at the Pier House—and then let's go back to the *Agualinda* and do wicked things to each other."

Don's face broke into a broad smile. Giving his wife a quick hug, he said, "I knew I didn't leave the real Meg Duncan back in Washington. Sounds like a great agenda, darling. Especially the last part. Maybe we should do the last part first."

"If we do the last part first, it'll be the only part," Meg said, laughing. "Besides, I want to enjoy a couple of hours of anticipation."

"Haven't we had enough deferred desire in our life?" Don asked huskily. His fingers cupped her elfin chin, then slid down the satin slope of her throat, hooking themselves in the vee of her open-necked blue cotton shirt.

"Don!" Meg protested, her color rising. But a quick glance around the crowded bar told her that its denizens were too busy eating, drinking, laughing, and nuzzling their own companions to pay any attention to her.

Pretending to work open one of Meg's shirt buttons, Don said with a sigh, "Thank God you're as wild in private as you're chaste in public." He released his hold on her and reached up to brush back his shock of brown hair.

Meg watched a woman with cascading silvery locks laughingly feed French fries to a man who looked to be half her age. At another table on the screened-in porch adjoining the bar, two tanned blond men were whispering conspiratorially, their rippling chest muscles visible under their body-hugging T-shirts as they leaned toward each other. Through the front door came a group of nautical types, one of the men wearing a raffish bandana, pirate-style, and the lone woman in a red bikini, a dozen gold chains, and nothing else except her honeyed tan.

"Do you wish I was wild in public, too?" Meg asked. "Want me to walk around in a red bikini?"

"You've got the figure for it." Don grinned. Then, swooping her into a hug that threatened to unseat her, he said, "Hey, we've never been in the business of trying to change each other, and I don't see any reason to start now. I love you the way you are."

"You did say back on the *Agualinda* that you wished I'd wear halters and shorts," Meg pointed out.

"Sure—for my consumption. I didn't say the whole world had to be given access to the goods, did I? I love the way you look in sheer nightgowns, but I don't ever remember suggesting you wear one to a party." Forcing his face into a scowl, urging thunder into his voice, Don added, "If you ever wear a red bikini in public, I'll tan your fanny, young woman."

"If I ever wear a bikini in public, my fanny will be the only untanned part of me." Meg giggled.

Lovingly linking arms, they sipped out of each other's beer mugs, then tore into the basket of sizzling conch fritters that Flip put in front of them.

As she tasted the unique combination of sweet, briny conch and peppery batter, Meg felt contentment take possession of her body and being. Uncle Win's ghost seemed to be happily smiling on her and Don. Memories of the *Agualinda*'s dampness and roller-coaster motion receded like an unpleasant dream. Her anxieties about Don and herself floated off to sea.

"I love you," she told Don—the abiding truth, the only truth that mattered.

"Enough to give me the last fritter?" he asked, reaching toward the all-but-empty basket.

She grabbed his hand. "Enough to order another basket—and share it with you," she returned with a smile.

As he opened his mouth to retort, she fed him the fritter in question, then stole some of it back with a searing, searching kiss.

# Chapter 5

T HWARTED AT EVERY TURN!" Meg exclaimed with a good-natured sigh as they approached the brick wall at 907 Whitehead Street. A young redheaded woman of about eighteen was shooing out a group of reluctant tourists and resolutely locking the wrought-iron gate.

Meg looked longingly past the giraffe-necked date palms and leafy-fronded palmettos at the Spanish colonial stone house where Ernest Hemingway had written some of his most important novels. Somehow it seemed important to wander through the rooms that had once been his, to cross the courtyard behind the house to the second-story study where his typewriter sat in solitary splendor on a small table.

"It's five past five," the woman at the gate informed Meg firmly, glancing at her watch for confirmation. "I really can't let you in. Anyway, I'm talked out for the day," she added, putting a hand to her throat and smiling ruefully.

"Oh, we don't need the guided tour," Meg shot back, with the speed and insistence that had made her so formidable in a courtroom. "We've been here several times. We just want to pop in for a few minutes to touch base."

"We'll be open at nine in the morning," the woman said. "I'm sorry,

we're closed," she called out to a gray-haired couple who came hurrying up to the gate, their hot-colored, floral-patterned cotton garb pro-
claiming that they had already checked out another local attraction,
Key West Hand Print Fabrics.

"Closed!" the female half of the couple echoed in disbelief. She
turned on her husband. "Henry, it's your fault for spending all afternoon at that damn cigar shop."

With great ceremony, Henry extracted a seven-inch Churchill in
a natural wrapper from his breast pocket, twirling it solemnly before
returning it to its protective sleeve.

"I'm sure Papa Hemingway would have thought it more important
for me to have a good cigar than to see his house," he said, taking the
woman by the arm.

"You never understood Papa," the woman declared, reluctantly
allowing herself to be led away from the gate. "When my literary circle
read *A Farewell to Arms* and *The Sun Also Rises*, Phyllis Frank said I
was the embodiment of Hemingway's feminine ideal, and everyone
agreed."

As the couple drew out of earshot, Meg, Don, and the red-haired
young woman exchanged glances, then broke into whoops of laughter.
Impulsively the woman unlocked the gate.

"If you promise not to refer to Hemingway as Papa, I'll let you in,"
she said. "For ten minutes. Then I've got to go bail out my mother.
She runs a guest house around the corner on Truman Avenue, and
she's got a couple who offered to pay ten dollars an hour for a baby-
sitter, can you imagine? It's not just the money, though it will be
nice," the young woman added breathlessly. "It's that they're driving
my mother crazy."

As Don reached into his pocket, she waved away the idea of their
paying the admission fee. "I'll collect tomorrow. Or whenever you
come back. Besides," she said, winking at Meg, "you're the embodiment of Hemingway's feminine ideal."

Tacitly Meg and Don agreed to skirt the main house and head for
Hemingway's study in the back. Cats scampered out of their path,
some pausing to refresh themselves at the blue-and-white china bowls
that Hemingway had favored for his pets. Though she harbored no

more fondness for household menageries than she did for trees or birds, Meg felt the cats belonged here. The skinny gray kittens that abounded seemed somehow especially Hemingwayesque.

"Since when were you such a fan, anyway?" Don demanded as Meg gazed rapturously at the big old manual typewriter in the book-lined study.

Meg let her eyes travel around the sparse yet pleasantly chuttered room.

"He was such an *accomplisher*," she said, taking in a deep breath—feeling as if the air contained magic molecules.

Don nodded knowingly. "None of that Key West lolling about for Papa, right? Or at least when he lolled, it was grist for the mill." Putting his arm around Meg's slender waist, he added, "Maybe you should write a book about our time here. *Doing Nothing*, by Meg Duncan. It has a ring, don't you think? Then we could have our nothing and a something, too."

Meg turned to meet his tender gaze. "Am I hopeless? Doomed never to unwind?"

"Hopeless. But so absolutely adorable." He let his gaze travel the planes of her face. "You got some color out there, did you know that? A faint layer of tropical pink over your polite Washington tan." His fingers outlined the sun blush on her cheeks. His lips followed his fingers. "Nice. Awfully nice."

"Darling—"

"Shhh," Don commanded, his lips ardent against hers. His hands gripped her shoulders, pulling her against him, then slid possessively down her back to clasp the compact roundness of her derriere. "I want you."

"Now?" Meg's eyes widened. "Here?"

"Why not? It's not a temple, is it? Or maybe it is—a temple consecrated to Eros." Don deliberately turned her around so his hands could travel north, to the lush terrain of her breasts. The clean-cut, boyish features of his face took on a sensual shimmer. "Right here," he said with insistent softness, "where all those great love scenes were written."

Meg's breath caught in her throat. Don had the look she sometimes saw when they'd been forced to spend a week apart. Her blood beat out the rhythms of excitement—and fear. The moist, hot Florida air was menacingly still. Any minute they might be discovered. But she wanted him. God, she wanted him. He was her husband, hers by every right, yet somehow lusciously forbidden. Her nipples swelled insistently against her cotton shirt.

"That woman—" she began feebly.

"She's gone off to babysit and forgotten about us," Don said, his fingers beginning to unfasten her buttons. He probed urgently at the lacy bra beneath. "Meg, you're so lovely." Closing in to sear her lips with his, he rivaled the heat in the air with his steamy glance.

Her knees trembling, Meg arched her throat in invitation. "Don. My Don."

Suddenly the air was rent with panicky shouting. "Calliope! No! Come down!"

"What?" Meg and Don exclaimed in unison.

"Calliope!" they heard again, the voice unmistakably that of the young red-haired woman who'd opened the gate for them. "It's not safe! Come back down the stairs!"

"Oh, my God," Meg said, clutching Don out of anxiety now, not desire. "She must be on that old rope catwalk that Hemingway used to get from the main house to this building." Hastily buttoning her shirt, she ran to the French doors. A chain and stern warning sign were meant to deter the adventurous from using the now-frayed catwalk. Another chain and sign had been installed at the other end of the catwalk, too, but they hadn't kept Calliope from wandering out onto the alluring contraption.

Meg held her breath as the child took one step, then another, then grabbed the side rope for support as the catwalk swayed. The redhead had dashed up the wrought-iron stairs to the verandah, but just as she thrust out her arms to grab Calliope, the child took one more-step and moved out of reach.

Catching sight of Meg, the woman mouthed, "I don't dare go out on the rope. I don't think it will hold my weight."

Would the time-worn catwalk hold even Calliope's weight? Meg's stomach lurched as the child took another tentative step on the fragile structure. Even if the rope held fast, the little elf could easily slip through the wide-open weave of the treads.

"Calliope, darling, please, please come back," the redhead called out. "We'll feed the kittens. Doesn't that sound like fun?"

"I don't like animals," came the petulant response. Calliope moved defiantly forward. As Meg watched in horror, the child's sandaled foot slipped, and she lurched. Tears followed instantly. "I want my mommy," she wailed, grabbing the supporting rope. She crouched down on her precarious perch, ignoring all of her sitter's enticements.

"How about a swim with me?" Meg called out when there was a pause between sniffles.

Calliope instantly turned her head toward the far end of the catwalk, her eyes widening as she saw Meg and Don. "Hi!" she said brightly, checking her tears midstream. Meg might have been a once-dear friend, long lost, encountered anew at a cocktail party. "I knew I'd see you again. Can I go in without my water wings?"

"Have you learned how to swim since Coconut Grove?" Meg called out. She managed to keep her voice light and easy; only Don's steadying hands on her shoulders told the truth about how tense she was.

"Well, sort of," Calliope said. "I mean, I just pretend I'm a fish and then I never can drown."

"Well, we'll see about the wings," Meg said. "Maybe I can give you lessons."

"I'd love you to give me lessons because you're the best swimmer in the world," Calliope asserted. She got to her feet and made a move toward Meg.

"Back the other way," Meg ordered instantly. "It's shorter and it's safer."

"But—"

"No buts," Meg said sternly. "You go back the other way, or no deal."

Calliope gave forth an audible sigh. Then she turned without a word and scampered back to safety.

As soon as Meg and Don saw her in the arms of her sitter, they raced down the stairs from Hemingway's loft and across the fieldstone courtyard.

"How can I ever thank you?" the redhead said to Meg, as Calliope sailed up into the latter's arms. "Thank God I let you two in here. Are you friends of Calliope's parents? I bet you have a child her age. A dozen children! I never saw anyone so smart with kids."

"I just seem to know this kid," Meg said, making a little face. She set Calliope down. "I think some introductions are in order. I'm Meg Duncan," she said to the redhead. "This is my husband, Don."

"Hello! I'm Jane Albury."

"And this is the famous Calliope, Don," Meg went on. "Calliope, this is Don."

"Is he really your husband?" the child asked.

"Absolutely," Meg assured her.

"Well, I think he looks more like your busband."

Bowing deeply, Don said, "I am also her busband. And she is my bife."

"And you're my baby-bitter," Calliope said to Jane, over the grown-ups' laughter, "and I'm Balliope." She started hopping up and down. "When are we going bwimming, Meg? I mean, Beg?"

"Tomorrow," Meg said.

"Tomorrow!" Calliope echoed indignantly. Putting her hands on her little hips, she purposefully eyed the catwalk.

Six adult arms reached out to restrain her.

"Tomorrow," Meg repeated firmly. "And you're on probation until then, young lady. Any violations, and no swim." Her voice softening, she asked, "What shall it be—ocean, Gulf, or pool?"

"My mother's guest house has a lovely pool," Jane Albury offered. "And we've just put in a Jacuzzi. It's right around the corner, on Truman. The Sea Grape Lodge. We'd be delighted to have you swim as our guests. Where are you staying?"

"At the Agualinda Lodge," Meg said dryly. "*Sans* pool or Jacuzzi." Seeing puzzlement on Jane Albury's pleasant face, she amended, "The *Agualinda* is a houseboat moored over near the shrimp docks. We inherited it from my uncle. We moved in—can it be?—this afternoon." She shook her head as a montage of pictures flashed through her mind. "Don and I seem to have lived three or four entire lives today."

"Three or four entire *bives*," Don corrected her, to Calliope's delight. "And I for one could use a *brink*. Shall we head down to the Pier House?"

"That sounds heavenly," Meg said, remembering the gracious Gulf-side hotel and restaurant, with its terrace bar offering ringside views of the sunset. She turned to Calliope. "I'll see you at ten o'clock tomorrow morning at the Sea Grape," she said crisply. "In swim togs. Jane, will you check with Calliope's parents to make sure that's all right? I'll call you tonight to confirm."

"Oh, I know it's fine," Jane said. "Tomorrow's my day off here, and I already agreed to spend the morning with our little friend."

"It's a date then." Meg fixed her eyes on Calliope's face. "And no more shenanigans until then, do you hear? Do you know what she-nanigans are?"

"Well, they're different from *he*nanigans," Calliope said. "I bet if I were a boy, I'd do henanigans."

"I bet you would," Don exclaimed. To Meg's astonishment, he picked Calliope up, whirled her around, and planted a kiss on her forehead as he set her down. Then he linked arms with Meg and led her down Whitehead Street.

# Chapter 6

MEG SIPPED HER FROTHY, TANGY MARGARITA and let the sky fill her mind. Pinks and purples licked the underside of a single pure white layer of cloud, promising a dazzling sunset. Everywhere else there was blue, the color of peace. She closed her eyes and laid her head on Don's shoulder. The laughter and chatter of their fellow drinkers washed over her, an undemanding music. She felt lazy, sensual, happy.

"Chapter one," she murmured to Don. "First they did nothing on the verandah at the Pier House. They drank their drinks and did nothing. They sniffed the sea and looked at the clouds and did nothing. Meg closed her eyes and did nothing. Don looked at the pretty blond waitresses in their revealing flowered dresses . . . and he damn well better have done nothing."

Don's laughter chimed in with hers. "Papa Hemingway, move over," he said.

Meg licked salt off the rim of her glass, then took a small swallow of the drink. "I suspect I'm as talented at writing about doing nothing as I am at doing nothing."

"You don't have to be good at doing nothing," Don said. "That's the whole point. Nobody's judging. Nobody's even looking."

"You're looking," Meg returned.

"Just at how beautiful you are. My prerogative."

"After all these years?" Meg's fingers danced along Don's bare arm.

"Thank God there's no statute of limitations on a husband's infatuation," Don said.

"I don't know," Meg began meditatively. "I think you're aging better than I am. I saw a gray hair on my head this morning."

"You did?" Don studied her sleek brown hair. "Show me. I don't want to miss a major landmark like that."

"I pulled it out," Meg said.

"You're kidding me!"

"Nope. I pulled it out, burned it, and scattered the ashes."

"Meg—"

"All right, I pulled it out and flushed it down the toilet." She gave way to a giggle.

"That was a flagrant waste of a tankful of water," Don said sternly. "Dissipating one of our most precious national resources. You save the next hair for me, do you hear?"

"I hair," Meg said. The laughter rolled out.

A waitress noted their empty glasses and asked if they'd like another round.

"I want to go down to Mallory Square," Meg said, and Don nodded his agreement. The sky was growing more intense as sunset neared. Mallory Square, on the edge of the water, would be a carnival now.

They asked the waitress for their bill.

"Mine," Meg said when it came.

"Mine," Don said, covering the green-and-white bill.

Meg pretended to consider, as if their funds were separate and distinct. "Okay, but I get to take you to dinner."

"Only if I get to put a dollar in the hat of the first juggler we see." Don signed a traveler's check, gave it to the waitress, and said they wouldn't need change.

"Did I overtip?" he asked Meg, interpreting the look she gave him as they started down the wooden stairs.

"Of course. You've been overtipping like crazy ever since we got Win's money." She kissed him on the cheek.

"Do you suppose we'll always feel a little guilty about being rich?" Don asked.

"I hope so."

He squeezed her hand. "Maybe it's time to give away another chunk."

Before leaving Washington, they'd made a sizable donation to a shelter for homeless women, and they'd pledged smaller amounts to half a dozen different legal defense funds.

"I wish Calliope didn't come from a wealthy, family," Meg blurted out. "It would be fun to buy toys and clothes for her. But I have a feeling the last thing she needs is objects."

A barefoot, bearded man in running shorts danced up the wooden steps, brushing by them. The smell of beer rolled off him in waves. "Objects, objects," he sang. "Who has the objects? You got to travel light."

"You traveling light or lit?" Meg called out.

"Hey, she's all right!" the young man called back. "Light or lit, have you seen it?" He disappeared into the crowd above them.

"Thus Key West," Don said with an indulgent grin. "Shall we go back up to the Pier House and find that guy and offer to make him rich beyond his wildest dreams?"

Meg considered for a moment. "He's probably got a trust fund," she decided. "He could buy us and sell us a dozen times over. Those were state-of-the-art running shorts he was wearing."

"And he'd been drinking imported beer. I could tell by the richness of his breath. But to get back to Calliope—"

"That was silliness," Meg said decisively. "She doesn't need anything except new parents—and those we can't buy her."

"You really felt that strongly about them?"

Meg shrugged. "Maybe I'm just prejudiced against backgammon players. I don't know—they gave me a feeling I sometimes get when I'm in a courtroom listening to a witness—too smooth to be true. Or maybe it's that Calliope behaves the way I think kids behave when their parents don't do their job. But it's hardly my field of expertise. Oh, Don, look. Someone's juggling with fire in the Square."

As they joined the gaily dressed throng alongside the water,

Meg unfastened her sandals and put them in her bag. The concrete quay was not fabulous to walk on, but it still held the day's warmth, and going barefoot out of doors, in a crowd, gave Meg a thrill. Don smiled appreciatively as she wiggled her toes and let out a hum of pleasure.

The Duncans joined a thick circle of people cheering and applauding as a black-garbed juggler tossed flaming torches while pedaling a unicycle. Reminding Meg of their deal, Don put a dollar in the juggler's proffered hat, even though they'd only caught the end of the show.

Meg and Don moved on, gratefully inhaling the tangy air, exclaiming as the sun dropped beneath the cloud layer and hung naked in the sky, too brilliant for unshielded eyes to focus on.

They gave money and words of praise to a young woman stroking sweetness out of an autoharp as her toddler—wearing only a droopy diaper—munched a zwieback in time to her tunes.

They crouched at the edge of the quay to look down at a dinghy full of giant conch shells being hawked by a sunburned fisherman with the reddest, bushiest beard Meg had ever seen. The fleshy pearlescent pinks and scalloped edges of the shell called to something in her. To Don's surprise, and her own, Meg heard herself tell the fisherman she'd take that shell over there by the oar, the shell with the glow so rich it seemed to reflect the sunset.

"That one's special. I was going to save it," the fisherman said. "But for eight bucks I could be persuaded to part with it."

Meg didn't argue, though she'd seen other shells go for six dollars.

"Want me to gift wrap it?" the fisherman asked. He pointed to a pile of newspaper.

"No thanks." Meg smiled. She reached down for the shell, handing over money. "Is it really special?" she asked. "Can I hear the sea in it?"

The fisherman grinned. "You can hear a harp in it. You can hear—what do they call those steam-whistle organs they have for merry-go-rounds? A calliope."

Meg and Don looked at each other. Meg put the shell to her ear.

"I can hear the sea, but that's all." She smiled at the fisherman, not wanting him to think she was having second thoughts about the price. "I still think it's beautiful. Worth eight dollars."

"You'll hear the calliope," he insisted. "When you're ready."

Don put his arm around Meg as they walked away. "Was that your basic Key West mystical experience, or was it? Calliope indeed."

"I'd call it your basic coincidence," Meg said. "Like my shell?"

"It's gorgeous. But since when does Meg Duncan collect shells? You're aware, aren't you, that it's a natural object?"

"Don't be silly," she said. "That nice fellow in the boat made it. Anything this beautiful has to be man-made."

Don leaned over and very gently bit her ear. "You're a character, Mrs. Duncan. Oh, look, they're getting ready for the big show."

Everyone on the quay was facing the Gulf now, watching the scarlet orb of the sun begin its final descent below the horizon. A guitarist strummed a tense chord. A penny whistle sounded, its notes plaintive. A child called for its father.

"And now for my next act . . ." the juggler boomed out, as the sun sank into the sea.

The crowd applauded the sun.

Don put his hands on Meg's shoulders, his lips against her lips. She saw reflected fire in his brown eyes. "It's all about us," he murmured. "The sun, the shell, the music, the applause—everything."

She pressed a kiss into his words. She felt the truth in what he was saying. She told him how much she loved being alive—in his life.

"We're just beginning, do you realize?" Don tasted the corners of her mouth. "This is a better beginning than the first one because we're so beautifully sure of each other. We don't have to waste any time playing games. And yet . . ."

"What?" Meg asked as his voice trailed off.

"We still get to discover each other. All over again. We have the excitement without the anxiety. Do you feel that way, too, Meg?" His eyes searched hers. "I want you to feel it. Excited but not scared."

"I do," she returned fervently. It was as if all her earlier fears had sunk into the sea with the sun. She gave a contented sigh. "I wish this moment could last forever."

"It will last forever. That's the best part. It will last because it will change. Things that don't change die, but things that change just keep growing."

Meg stared at him as they turned their backs to the water and started toward Duval Street. "I never heard you talk this way before."

"It's the Key West influence," Don said lightly. "The same mysterious something in the air that made you want to buy a conch shell. Speaking of buying—did you offer dinner, or was I dreaming?"

Meg lifted her conch shell and addressed it. "Should I buy him dinner?" she asked. She held the shell to her ear. She listened. She nodded. She smiled. "It said the best is none too good for you. And suggested Cuban food. Shall we go to La Lechonera?"

Don offered his arm. "You're on."

# Chapter 7

A T DINNER THEY TALKED ABOUT BED. They decided to skip dessert, though both of them loved Cuban flan.

They walked back to the *Agualinda*, arms around each other's waists, pausing now and then to share a fevered kiss.

"Has it been weeks, months, years?" Meg asked breathily, stunned by the urgency of her desire.

"I feel that way, too," Don groaned. "Let's run."

Once through their front door, they stopped only to set down the fragile conch shell among their not-yet-unpacked luggage. Then they headed straight up the ladder to the sleeping platform and the firm cotton futon mattress which would be their bed. They knelt opposite each other, not quite touching, as though seeking one more round of the gorgeous agony of desire unfulfilled.

Don was a dim glow to Meg's eyes. She had never known such darkness. Sky and sea outside the window were varying shades of black. There had to be stars out there, but clouds obscured them. There had to be whitecaps, but one wave swallowed another too quickly for the white to register against the night.

Don asked if she wanted a light.

She shook her head, then laughed softly. How could he see the motion? "No. It's exciting. I never realized black came in so many colors."

Don's hands caught at her waist, gently pulling her away from the window. His hands traveled down to the taut curves of her hips, then paralleled each other down her thighs. A groan of pleasure escaped his lips.

In the covering darkness Meg felt as though their clothes were melting from their bodies. Outside the crashing of the waves sounded in the infinite night. She and Don were alone in the universe; they *were* the universe.

As Don pulled back the topsheet and quilt, she halfheartedly protested that she ought to go downstairs and brush her teeth so she wouldn't have to get up later.

"Don't be such a good little girl," Don whispered. "Beside, I want to taste the margaritas, and the *ropa vieja*, and the sea air . . ." His tongue gently probed at her lips. "Delicious. I want more."

"Garlic," Meg mumbled. La Lechonera had outdone itself in the herb and spice department.

Don unabashedly licked the corners of her mouth. "This isn't Washington. Garlic is allowed. I think it's kind of sexy." He invaded her mouth altogether now, until she was no longer sure whose tongue was whose, which breath was which.

The houseboat swayed, and Meg tensed, but Don murmured, "Go with it," and her body magically adjusted. She would go with everything. She would submit to the sea, and Key West, and most of all to Don.

The darkness made everything right. There weren't any borders, any walls.

Don seemed to sense her longing to surrender. He urged her back against the pillows, then imprisoned her wrists in his hands as he scorched her mouth with his fiery kiss. Not letting her move except to arch against him, he trailed kisses and gentle bites across her neck, then licked her earlobe and blew into her hair until she thought she would scream for need of him.

"You've got to let me go so I can hold you," she groaned. "My arms are desperate for you."

"Only your arms?"

"Every inch of me."

"I'm letting you go, but only because I have to put my hands on your breasts." Don released her wrists, then caressed the creamy globes, his fingers dancing with wonder. "The most beautiful body in the world," he said. "These are the nipples of fantasy." He knelt over her and put his mouth where his hands had been.

Meg felt her whole body and being center in one nipple, then the other, as he tongued the sweetly aching flesh to hardness.

Don spun his body over hers with his athlete's grace so that his chest, his belly, his muscular thighs could graze the softness and hardness of Meg's breasts. Even his toes got their moment, and Meg's laughter didn't undercut the strangely thrilling sensation.

"I want you so many different ways, I'm going crazy," he whispered. "Tell me what will please you the most."

"Anything. Everything, darling. Do it all. Let me do it all to you."

He ran his tongue from the valley between her breasts to the mystery of her navel to the secret world at the joining of her thighs. Her blood was a river of fire, her breath a jagged drumbeat in her own ears.

"How's that for everything?" Don asked.

For answer, she thrust her hands into the warmth of his hair. She imprisoned his legs with her own.

From the brink of the abyss, she called out that she had to let her mouth have the freedom of his body before she went over the edge. Eager as a gazelle, she took the top side now. Her tongue, lips, and teeth made dessert of his sweet flesh. Every hillock of muscle, every thicket of hair was a separate sweet on her palate.

"I have to have you—now," Don cried, and the cry was for her moment, too.

Side by side, eternal partners, all jousting behind them, they joined in ultimate union. The *Agualinda* seemed to pitch and yaw, but Meg knew the storm was inside her. Clutching Don, she happily drowned, knowing they'd fall through the bottom of the sea and be reborn.

Afterward, they lay snugly against each other, not speaking for long, peace-filled moments. Finally a buoy clanged, breaking the crystalline mood.

Don moved slightly away. "Want to do it again?"

"Mmph." Meg threw a pillow at him. "What if I said yes, big shot?"

"At your service, ma'am."

"Well, I think I *will* brush my teeth this time," Meg said. "Et cetera. Assuming I'm in shape to make it down the ladder."

"While you're down there, bring me some cola with ice?"

"We never did go shopping today," Meg reminded him, tentatively reaching for the first rung. "Unless Flip thought of leaving a bag of ice in the freezer."

"Knowing Flip, I bet he did. I wouldn't want to count on him for orange juice—but I bet there's ice and plenty of beer."

"And eggs, and English muffins, and butter, and grape jelly," Meg called up from the little kitchen. "And orange juice. Stale-dated sometime next century."

"Well, sure. No one drinks fresh orange juice in Florida, hadn't you noticed? They consider it unpatriotic. Oranges are money. Damn nice of Flip, in any event. I'm glad we don't have to go out for breakfast because I want to make love to you twice tomorrow morning. Once before breakfast, once after."

Meg came back up the ladder, bearing a clanking glass of soda. "Even though we're doing it again tonight?"

"Even though," Don said. "And we're going to make love tomorrow afternoon and evening too. Pausing only to teach Calliope how to swim and buy a different flavor of jam."

Meg felt stung. It was almost as though he had mentioned another woman's name in the midst of their intimate spree. She shook off the unworthy feeling and sank down onto the futon. Don had lit a small bedside lamp that Win had made by glueing shells to an empty bottle of beer and adding a socket and wires; she looked at Don in the soft pink gleam made by the low-watt bulb. His air of serenity moved her. She touched him and said, "Hi."

"Alone at last." A daffy look of fondness crossed his face. He took a sip of soda, then leaned forward to run a chilly tongue down the brief slope of Meg's pert nose.

"That tickles," she protested, giggling. She dove under the quilt, burying her head.

"I'm going to get you," Don said.

Meg felt motion above her as his hand burrowed under the quilt. An ice cube made contact with a buttock and she shrieked. "You— you—" she spluttered, coming out from under the quilt. "I'll never get you soda with ice again, you rat."

He made a little-boy pout. "Aw, please, Mrs. Duncan. Just once?"

"Just once what?" she asked suspiciously. She sat up, folding her arms across her breasts.

"Well, you see," Don began, "my wife was so cravenly hungry for my body that she made me leave the restaurant tonight without dessert." His brown eyes flashed. "And I thought—"

"Your wife made *you* leave!" Meg retorted indignantly. "I seem to remember your saying that no flan could be as sweet as her—"

"Be that as it may, counselor," Don said, "the fact remains: I didn't get dessert. And I thought that, being as how we're in the tropics—"

"Semitropics," Meg corrected.

"Being as how we're where it's hot, I'd like some kind of frozen dessert." He retrieved the ice cube he'd dropped back into the glass of cola. "I understand this restaurant serves sublime popsicles. Pink ones—all natural. I'd like to order a matched pair." Brandishing his ice cube, he eyed her nipples intently.

"I don't know," Meg began, not uncrossing the arms she'd protectively wrapped over her breasts. "What's in it for me?"

Don leered. "Ecstasy beyond your wildest dreams." The ice cube dripped a drop onto the quilt. "This offer may not last. Void where taxed or prohibited by law."

Meg slowly dropped her arms, then cupped her left breast and offered it to her husband. He reverently kissed the creamy flesh, then unceremoniously touched the ice cube to the scarlet nipple.

Meg squealed, but it was a squeal of pleasure; her body somehow translated cold into heat. And Don's mouth was instantly where the ice had been, adding heat to heat, pleasure to pleasure.

Now Meg was the eager one. "The other side," she said. "It's jealous." She offered her right breast.

Don looked up, an embarrassed grin crossing his lean, clean-featured face. "I spilled my soda." He moved aside to reveal a large wet spot in the middle of the bed. "I'll change the sheets," he offered. "I guess we'll have to put down a towel over the wet spot on the futon. Unless Flip thought ahead and put down a protective plastic cover."

"If he did, I'll strangle him," Meg said cheerfully. She opened a built-in cupboard next to the bed. "Don!" she exclaimed, as she looked inside.

Half a dozen sheet and pillowcase sets, pristine in their plastic wrappings, were lying on top of the handsome but somewhat worn linens that Win Carruthers had used. There was a note; Meg withdrew it, her hands trembling.

"Dearest children," she read to Don. "Happy second honeymoon. Happy new marriage. I leave here in great contentment knowing you will be coming. Enjoy each other. Enjoy it all. Remember: Life's too mysterious; don't take it serious. Love, Win."

Her eyes filled with tears, and Don's did too, but the tears hung unshed; weeping would have been an insult to the extraordinary man who'd written that note. Meg took out the new linen, exclaiming over the lace-trimmed ivories, the delicate floral patterns.

"He must have sent to one of the old Boston stores for these," she said. "Key West may sell the world's greatest bikinis, but I don't think it does much trade in linens of this caliber."

They unwrapped one of the packages because Don said the pale peach tone reminded him of Meg's skin, and they remade the bed. The towel they'd folded over the wet spot on the futon made a lump in the middle, but they didn't mind. They were content to huddle next to each other in a narrow space. It wasn't a night for escaping into privacy.

"This has been one of the extraordinary days of my life," Meg mumbled sleepily, settling against the sublimely familiar contours of Don's body. "So much old and so much new, all sort of coming together. I feel as though I've changed dramatically, but I'm more myself than ever. Do you know what I mean?"

"I do," Don said, holding her close. "I think it started for me when we left Washington. It didn't hit me all at once the way it did you—but yes."

Meg was silent for a moment. "Are we going to be happy forever and ever?" she asked.

"We are," Don said firmly. "With our full share of lumps and bumps in between the moments of truth and beauty."

"It's not fair." Meg sighed, feeling her body starting to slip into sleep but needing to finish the thought. "We know everything now. We should be permanently happy."

"Then we'd forget the value of happiness," Don said. Hugging her tight against him, he tenderly stroked her belly. "God, I love you, Meg."

They neglected to drop the bamboo blind on the window, and the light woke them at six. But they didn't mind at all. They just rewrote their agenda for the morning and made love twice before the English muffins.

# Chapter 8

MEG AND DON PAUSED ADMIRINGLY in front of the gleaming white three-storied house topped with a gabled roof and dormer windows. The Sea Grape Lodge spoke of loving care. The black shutters might have been painted the day before. The American flag flying from the second-floor balcony was bright and crisp. The verandah had plainly been swept within the hour, and the steps leading up to it recently scrubbed.

"That's a ficus tree," Don said, pointing to a massive trunk crowned with a shower of oval leaves. He paused, as if waiting to see if Meg would protest this further evidence of his unnatural interest in nature, but she just nodded and stared at the giant. "Isn't it incredible?" he went on. "That's one of the biggest I've seen."

"What are those hairy ropes?" Meg asked, pointing to the masses of matter dangling from the widespread branches.

"Those are aerial roots. If they're not cut, they enter the ground. One of these trees can practically make its own forest."

"It's too spooky to be beautiful," Meg said, shivering a little, "but it certainly is impressive." She surveyed the dramatic landscaping in front of the house, indicating an electric green fanlike arrangement of long-stemmed palm leaves about seven feet tall. "That's more my style."

Don nodded knowingly. "Because it's so sculptural it looks man-made, right?"

"Oh, you—" Meg began, then laughed and agreed. "Right."

"It's called the traveler's palm. The base of it holds water."

Meg took in the house, the greens, the occasional splashes of lemon yellow and shocking pink among the otherworldly shapes and dimensions of the densely planted trees. The air was rich with a sugary scent she recognized—on a previous visit; they'd toured the Key West Fragrance and Cosmetic Factory. "Frangipani," she said.

"On you it smells good," Don said. He pointed to a tree with long, elegantly oval leaves and pink, fivepetaled flowers. "There it is."

"You really don't like the smell?"

"It's just too relentlessly sweet. I like a little vinegar with my honey." He put his arm around Meg's shoulders and gave a squeeze. "That's why I like your personality so much, my darling."

Meg stuck out her tongue, then gave him a saccharine smile.

"Exactly," Don said.

A tanned young woman carrying a tennis racquet came out the front door of the Sea Grape Lodge and started down the sidewalk, wishing Meg and Don a good morning as she passed them.

"It's a rough life here, isn't it?" Don observed.

"We ought to try to play tennis today," Meg said, but in such a lazy voice that she and Don both burst into merry peals of laughter.

Meg pulled the bell next to the front door. A handsome red-haired woman in her late forties, trimly clad in a long-sleeved flowered shirt and white slacks, greeted them.

"You're Meg and Don, I bet," she said warmly, opening the door. "I'm Pooh Albury. Priscilla for real, but we Conchs have a passion for nicknames. At least my generation does. Jane is just Jane. She said you were fantastic with Calliope yesterday." Lowering her voice as she ushered them into a drawing room appointed with vintage wicker furniture, she added, "Which is more than I can say for her parents. Jane and Calliope are out back. I don't suppose you want to eat just before swimming, but a small coffee, perhaps? Elena, who cooks for me, makes the best Cuban coffee on the island."

"I never say no to Cuban coffee," Meg said.

"*Con leche?*" Pooh Albury inquired.

"No; black for us both, please, and not too sweet," Don said.

"You've been married for a while, I see," Pooh observed crisply. "My own marriage lasted long enough to produce Jane—but not long enough for me to be able to order coffee for my husband with any certainty he'd be pleased with the result." She walked through an arched doorway at the far end of the room, leaving Meg and Don to look wonderingly at each other.

"I like her," Meg decided instantly, though she'd been known to have allergic reactions to people who were too quick to tell their intimate stories. "Too bad she and Uncle Win never met, though she's a generation younger."

"How do you know they didn't meet?"

"Because Win would have dragged her off to the *Agualinda* after fifteen minutes! She's everything poor Aunt Carlotta wanted to be— social, attractive, strong—but Carlotta had no real guts. She was bred to be ladylike; nothing else mattered. Pooh Albury is a lady to her toes, but she's also, well, a helluva broad. Win would have loved the combination."

Smiling affectionately, Don brushed a kiss across Meg's lips. "What a character you are! A lady, a broad, a little girl, the world's most stellar woman. Have I told you how much I love you?"

"Tell me again," Meg entreated. "I promise I won't be bored."

Don was talking about love, and the making of love, when Pooh Albury returned with a wicker tray boasting three thimble-sized cups. Meg sighed contentedly at her first sip of the dark, syrupy coffee. She felt her adrenaline surge.

"It's too good," she said with another sigh. "It ought to be illegal."

"It once was," Don reminded her. "For some religious groups, it still is. Fantastic," she said to their hostess. "Would your cook—"

He was interrupted as a tall, silver-haired man in a khaki suit strode into the room, generating sparks of anger. "Pooh," he began, then stopped when he saw Meg and Don. "The Dauntless Duncans," he boomed. "I knew we'd meet again."

Meg recognized him instantly. Intercepting Don's puzzled look, she quickly said, "Do you remember my telling you about my seatmate on the plane trip down here last December? This is Victor Green."

The men shook hands.

"You two did leave the Justice Department, right?" Victor Green said. "That wasn't just a rumor?"

"We really truly did it," Meg confirmed, making a note in her mental file that the silver-haired defense attorney looked relieved. "We're on an extended vacation. Do we dare ask about you?"

"Meg and Don came to take Calliope for a swim," Pooh Albury quickly supplied, as though this were information Victor Green had better have.

"Calliope. Our beloved Calliope," Victor said with a grin. "She surely has a knack for making friends. How did you happen to meet?"

"She decided to drown one day in Coconut Grove and I decided differently," Meg said. Her mind made a little leap. "Are her parents clients of yours?"

Victor Green smiled enigmatically. "Beautiful day, isn't it?" he said.

"Glorious," Don answered, "and I think we ought to head for the pool. This is beginning to feel like a Washington encounter. Thanks for the coffee, Mrs. Albury. Do we go out that way?"

"Yes, and call me Pooh, for heaven's sake."

"Don't let my abrasive ways get you down, kid," Victor said, clapping Don on the shoulder. "Meg tell you I offered her a job? For both of you?"

"She told me," Don said stiffly. "We're not in the job market." He urged Meg out through the arched doorway.

Another door took them outside. The landscaping behind the house rivaled the brilliant trees and shrubs in the front, but Meg was too angry at Don for being so rude to ask for names, or even let him know how much the vista pleased her eye.

"Why were you so curt to Victor Green?" she demanded.

"I didn't like him," Don replied. "I didn't like the way he talked to us, and I didn't like the way he looked at you. Did he make a pass at you on the plane?"

"Oh, Don." Meg could see Calliope and Jane down at the oval

pool, and she knew they saw her and Don, but the moment had to be resolved before she could move. "He came on a little, but he's the kind of man who comes on with every woman. Nothing the remotest bit serious. He's a superb lawyer."

"He's a publicity seeker," Don returned, unyielding. He folded his arms across his chest. "The needs of his clients are incidental. He goes for the jazzy cases, then plays them for all they're worth."

Meg felt a headache starting, the first one since they'd given notice at the Department of Justice. Half of her wanted to ruffle Don's hair and tease him out of his temper; the other half wanted to do battle and prove her point.

She heard the contentious side of herself speak, without being aware of having made a conscious choice. "You go back and reread his appeal brief in *U.S. v. Hernandez*. He'd done his homework so meticulously, it was boring. Citation after citation. But damned good law."

"I think you like him," Don said incredulously, as though Meg had just announced her affection for some creepy crawly insect.

"Well, I don't dislike him," she snapped back. "I thought our new life was supposed to be full of wonder and growth and change. I didn't hear the part about making snap judgments and being rude and embarrassing me."

"You embarrassed *me*," Don said. "All that stuff about your dear old seatmate. It didn't take you ten seconds to remember him. Been thinking about him since last December?"

"Oh, sure," Meg said with heavy sarcasm. "I had Uncle Win leave us the *Agualinda* because I figured that was the best way for me to run into Victor again. Wasn't it obvious last night and this morning that I was mooning over some other man? Thank God we—"

"All right, all right," Don interrupted, suddenly sheepish. "I guess I got a little carried away there. I'm sorry."

Meg said she accepted his apology, and kissed him on the nose to give substance to her words. They held hands as they walked toward the pool and Calliope and Jane. Still, an unpleasant buzz sounded faintly inside Meg's head; her heart was no longer dancing the jig that had set its rhythm half an hour ago.

Jealousy had never surfaced, not once, during the Duncans' many separations over the years. It was as though distance had only served to heighten their awareness of the bond between them. Sometimes the work had seemed incidental to their travels; they left each other from time to time so their bodies could sweetly sting with the need for reunion.

Although Meg knew husbands and wives who heightened their attraction for each other by creating jealousy, she and Don had never found jealousy to be anything but ugly. So why Don's strange, harsh reaction to Victor Green—the insinuation that Meg might not have despised his advances?

The disturbing question was put aside as Calliope came running across the grass and tackled Meg's knees.

"Where's your swim togs?" Calliope demanded, eyeing Meg's khaki skirt and madras shirt.

"Underneath," Meg assured her.

"Then where's your undies?" the blond tyke pressed.

Meg laughed. "In my bag. With my towel. You'd make a good mother."

"I am a good mother." Calliope's turquoise eyes sparkled. "I have two dolls and a pig, and I'm their excellent mother. I never spank them, and I don't make them clean their room, and I never play backgammon when they need me."

Meg watched bemused as Don crouched down to be on a level with Calliope.

"Tell me, excellent mother, what are your dolls' names?" He slipped an arm around the child's waist.

Calliope fixed her eyes on Don, Meg, and Jane in turn. A thumb went into her mouth. "It's my special secret. Promise you won't tell anyone, not even my parents?"

Meg disliked the idea of coming between a child and her parents—even parents she herself didn't admire—but hadn't the Supreme Court upheld the idea that minors had rights of privacy?

"If it's a secret, maybe you shouldn't tell us," Meg hedged the bet.

A small foot was stamped. A small mouth pouted, extruding a thumb. "I want to tell you. They're *my* babies, and I can tell you if I want to. The boy baby is Antonio and the girl is Maria, and the pig is named Salsicha. That means 'sausage' in Portuguese, though I would never eat him, not even if I was starving."

Meg nodded. She remembered that Calliope's father, though not her mother, had spoken with a faint Brazilian inflection. Portuguese would be his native tongue, then. "Those are lovely names," she told Calliope.

"You promise you won't tell anyone?" Looking stricken, Calliope clung to Meg's thigh.

"I promise that we absolutely won't tell anyone."

"Cross your heart and hope to die, stick a needle in your eye?"

The three grown-ups promised.

"Well, are we going to stand around all day, or are we going swimming?" Meg demanded.

"Swimming!" Calliope shouted.

As Meg shucked her outer layer of clothing, she felt a sense of well-being wash over her again. All traces of her headache vanished. The clear air and strong sun were a kind of benediction. And though the junglelike shapes and colors and smells of the surrounding trees didn't give her the rush that an urban skyline did, they infused her with a measure of peace no city had ever bestowed. Then again, she'd never sought peace; she'd looked for the opposite. For a tiny, frightening instant she was caught in a tug-of-war: she wanted peace; she feared peace—wanted; feared. Then a swirl of breeze rustled the exotic leaves around her and swept the fear out of her heart. Peace needn't mean staleness and boredom and the end of accomplishment. She could have it both ways, and she would.

Don stripped down to his brief striped swimming trunks, and she felt all the rush she needed.

"My suit's back at the house," Jane Albury said. "Why don't I run up and change and—"

She was interrupted by her mother, hailing her from the back door, telling her she was wanted on the phone.

"Don't wait for me," the younger redhead said. "I have a feeling I know who's calling." She sprinted toward the house.

"Oh, boy," Calliope exclaimed. "Now we can play Fish family. I'm Baby Fish, and you're Mommy Fish"—she pointed to Meg—"and you're Daddy Fish," she said, poking Don in the bellybutton.

"Very finny." He glowered, then picked her up and swung her around. "No poking, do you hear?"

Meg left them to their roughhouse game and conspiratorial laughter. She walked down to the edge of the oval pool. A single frangipani blossom—she recognized it now—floated on the tranquil turquoise surface. She felt pleased with herself for knowing the name of the flower, then laughed at her own pleasure.

"What's up, darling?" Don called out.

"Oh, I just caught myself accomplishing, that's all. Admit it, Duncan," she added, "that's the whole point of being able to identify trees and plants rather than just responding to them with your senses. You feel as though you're *doing* something."

"Do you suppose?" he mused, heading toward the pool with Calliope astride his shoulders. "I guess the true do-nothing spirit wouldn't permit cataloguing. Somehow I just seem to be better able to enjoy the beauty of a flower if I know its name. It's a deep instinct, isn't it? Look at the way children name their dolls and stuffed animals and always want to know what things are called."

"I speak, therefore I am." Meg felt her smile widen as she looked at him standing there, his trimness and vitality on display in the brilliant light. His biceps rippled as he reached up to steady his restless rider. Meg wanted him again—carnally, quickly. She turned away to conceal her sizzling thoughts from Calliope. But she made herself a promise: she would make love with Don outdoors, in daylight if possible, and soon.

"I want to swim," Calliope announced imperiously, "and I want to swim now."

"Is that so?" Meg returned, putting her hands on her hips.

Don swung Calliope down. "I want to swim, *por favor*," he edited.

The golden head swiveled. "Do you speak Portuguese?"

"A few words. I speak a few words in a lot of languages."

"Are you a teacher?"

"A lawyer," Don said, then shook his head. "I used to be a lawyer," he corrected himself.

"Uncle Victor's a lawyer," Calliope said excitedly. "I want to be a lawyer when I grow up. Can girls be lawyers?"

"Girls can be anything they want to be," Meg said.

"Except fathers," Don cut in dryly.

Meg made a face. "I'm a lawyer, too, Calliope," she said, deliberately using the present tense. She was dying to ask Calliope what her parents' professions were—international backgammon hustlers, perhaps?—but she felt she'd inadvertently learned more about them than she should have, as it was. "What do you say we all be swimmers for the moment? I checked the pool, and the shallow end is really shallow. You don't have to wear your water wings as long as we're in there together."

Calliope jumped up and down for joy, her shimmering green one-piece suit flashing neon in the sun.

"But absolutely no fooling around in the water," Meg went on. "Swimming is serious business. Fun," she amended, as Calliope's face went sour, "but it can't be careless fun." She held out a hand. "In we go."

They walked down three broad steps into the shallow end of the oval, Calliope squealing happily about the coldness though Meg thought it warm. The water came to Calliope's breastbone. Meg guided her to the rim of the pool and showed her how to hold on.

"We're going to start with kicking," Meg said. "I bet you're a great kicker."

Don, standing above them, smiled and said, "I can testify to that." He bent down and rubbed a shin. "Will it disturb you serious swimmers if I dive in at the other end? Or maybe I'll try out the Jacuzzi. Unless that small round pool over there is just for waders."

"It's the funnest place!" Calliope said. "The water squirts you like anything. It tickles like crazy. I want to go in with you. Can I press the button?" She let go of the rim of the pool and turned toward the steps.

"What about your swimming lesson?" Don quickly asked, as though gauging the hurt Meg felt. "Meg is one of the all-time great swimming teachers. She taught me how to swim."

"Aw, I bet she didn't."

"She did."

"Didn't."

Meg contemplated swimming underwater to the far end of the pool and sneaking away. Would, anyone notice? But of course she couldn't leave Calliope alone in the pool, even with Don hovering attentively over her. She shook her head, as though to disperse the foreign, unwelcome feelings that had invaded her core. What on earth was happening to her?

Just as Don started into the pool to forestall the move to the Jacuzzi, Jane Albury came running down from the house, still clad in her bluejeans and strapless red gauze top.

"I knew it," she exclaimed. "Laura Spotswood decided to have her baby today. Which means they want me to fill in for her at the Hemingway House, even though it's my day off. Could you two possibly look after Calliope until two? Her parents have to go off to some kind of appointment, and they said it would be fine with them if you take the gig. Otherwise, I'll bring her to Hem's place, but . . ." She didn't have to finish her sentence to remind Meg and Don how well Calliope had done there the day before.

"Was there anything else you had in mind to do?" Don asked Meg, clearly delighted with the proposition.

She shook her head stiffly. "No, it's fine with me," she said, forcing warmth into her voice for the sake of flustered Jane. "We'll have a swim and maybe a trip to the aquarium or something, and of course we'll have lunch. There has to be lunch. And have you been on a houseboat?" she asked Calliope.

The child's eyes widened. Swimming pool eyes, Meg thought; they were the only truly turquoise eyes she'd ever seen, twins to the water. "It's my favorite book," Calliope exclaimed, the words rushing out. "*Tommy Lives on the Water*. And there's a bathroom and kitchen and everything. Could we have lunch on your houseboat? Could we? I'll wash my hands and help clean up and everything." She waded back to Meg and hugged her. "Can I bring my dolls and pig?"

Don's laughter forced Meg to meet his eyes. She realized how foolish she'd been to feel hurt when Calliope turned her attention to him. The kid obviously made a habit of playing her parents off against each other. Maybe all kids did.

How confusing the whole business of children was; how many fragilities were involved. She breathed a sigh of relief that she and Don had steered clear of the whole sticky business. Only why was she bending to scoop Calliope up? Why was she suddenly yearning to hold the wet little body? Their bathing suits made a squishy sound as they rubbed against each other, and the assembled company laughed.

"We'll be fine, obviously," Meg assured Jane. "You go do whatever you have to do. We'll bring Calliope back at two. Should we all see her parents off, or have they left?"

"They left," Jane said, and Meg had to give the little body in her arms another squeeze. Her mind raced back through time and she dwelled, for a terrible moment, on the memory of the day when she'd learned of her parents' death. She'd felt sorrow, shock, rage at the unfair world; most of all, she'd felt abandoned. And she'd been fifteen, very much her own young woman. She sensed, or imagined she sensed, that Calliope, barely five, felt that abandonment in miniature.

Maybe all kids looked wrenched when their parents took off, if only to go out for dinner, because their instincts told them that every separation was a rehearsal for irreparable loss.

"Meg?" Don's voice brought her back to the present. He was wading into the pool, concern all over his face. Her heart suffused with warmth as she realized he'd guessed where her thoughts had fled for an instant. His sheltering arms were around her and Calliope; he was suggesting they all warm up with some action or else get out of the pool.

Meg heard herself say something about wanting Calliope to kick, but at the same time her mind strove to finish a thought:

Maybe she'd been afraid to have children because she remembered all too well how much pain there could be in childhood. But one might as sensibly decline to fall in love on the grounds that all love meant loss. Marriage was, in part, the selection of one's eventual chief mourner. She'd known enough not to flee romantic love. Had she been wrong to flee the love of children?

She kissed Calliope's golden cheek. "Lunch on the houseboat," she said. "For child, dolls, pig, and all."

# Chapter 9

T HE AGUALINDA ROCKED AND ROLLED. The hamburgers sizzling in the frying pan sent forth a pungent odor. Meg nibbled a saltine in an effort to steady her belly against the twin assaults.

"I'm starved!" Calliope called from the loveseat where she was cutting up Win's old copies of the *Atlantic* under Don's watchful eyes.

Meg looked at the clock on the range: not quite yet noon. And Calliope had reportedly downed a huge breakfast. Just as well she was starving, in any event; it would probably take a very hearty appetite to face Meg's cooking. She looked dubiously at the plump patties, smacked them down with the back of the spatula, then flipped them over.

"They smell delicious," Don said, exaggerating each syllable. "I don't know why we've been eating in restaurants all these years."

"I'm tired of restaurants," said Calliope, sounding for all the world like a world-weary socialite whose name had appeared in too many gossip columns.

"Me, too," Meg heard Don say over the sound of slick paper being scissored to ribbons.

*Traitor!* Meg wanted to say, but she bit back the words. *Why aren't you cooking lunch? Why didn't you learn to cook all the years we dined à la credit card?* She didn't utter those words either.

She was the one who'd volunteered to cook hamburgers when Calliope had requested them. She was the one who'd eschewed ready-made frozen patties on the grounds that they didn't look wholesome. She, who had stared down hardened criminals in the awesome setting of a courtroom, wasn't about to be cowed by a pound of ground round.

The shameful truth, she admitted to herself as she got plates out of the cupboard, was that she wanted credit from Calliope for lunch. Of course she'd have to take the blame if it didn't work out.

How did you check the doneness of hamburgers, anyway, without hacking them to pieces?

The kitchen was too small to admit a table, so she put the plates, silverware, and napkins on a large pewter tray that Win had brought down from Boston. Then she added a salt shaker, a pewter pepper mill (dear Win with his elegant touches), and the bottle of ketchup Calliope had grabbed in the supermarket. The English muffins left over from breakfast went into the toaster; Meg refused to eat the cotton-wool creations known as hamburger rolls. She looked for a scraper to clean the carrots she'd bought. Finding none, she improvised with a paring knife. Two carrots down, one to go, and—ouch! She cut her finger. The wounded digit went into her mouth. She tasted blood.

"Don't overcook those burgers," Don called from the living room.

Meg slammed into the bathroom and got a Band-Aid. It would serve Don right if she leaked, and he got blood instead of ketchup with his lunch.

Returning to the kitchen, she put ice cubes in three glasses and poured orange juice. She looked at the tray and stuck her tongue out at it. The meal looked like an illustration from some goody-goody magazine for parents; the carrots and the orange juice were positively vulgar in their glow. What she really wanted for lunch was a grown-up club sandwich and vodka and tonic in a wood-paneled joint where the lights were low and jazz ruled the sound waves. And someone out of sight to do the dishes.

"I only drink orange juice for breakfast," Calliope announced as Meg marched in with the tray. "Can I have Coke as a special treat?"

Meg glared. "It's orange juice or nothing."

Calliope stamped a small foot. "Then I'll take nothing."

"Ah, there's nothing like lunch with two imperious women." Don sighed. "You two deserve each other." Holding an imaginary glass in one hand and an imaginary bottle in the other, he made a pouring motion. "Coming up, one big glass of nothing. And for you," he said to Meg, "a vodka and tonic?"

She had to grin. "How did you know?"

"Didn't I know how you wanted your coffee this morning?" He bit into his hamburger. "Didn't you know how I wanted my hamburger? Have we been married a decade for nothing?"

"Is it really okay?" Meg picked up her own hamburger.

"It's perfect. Juicy and delicious. How about yours, Calliope?"

"Delicious and juicy," the little girl said. She added a large dollop of ketchup and took a second bite. "It happens to be the best hamburger I ever ate."

"Happens to be—nothing," Don said. "This hamburger didn't just happen, it was created. By the multifaceted Meg Duncan, who's been hiding a talent all these years." He stood up. "One vodka and tonic coming up for the best little cook in Key West. The booze is under the sink, isn't it?"

"I didn't check, but that's where it always was. Finish your lunch, though. I'll be happy with orange juice."

"Me too," Calliope said unexpectedly.

They all clinked glasses.

After lunch Calliope got out her dolls and pig. Meg was astonished by the artistry evident in the toys; they appeared to have been carved by a master and dressed by one, too, down to handmade lace on Maria's skirt, perfect miniature buttons on Antonio's shirt, and a splendid polka-dot bow around Salsicha's curly tail. She was almost sorry when Calliope asked if she could bring the toys upstairs, but she gave permission in the interest of a spate of grown-up peace.

Don washed the dishes. They turned on the radio and found their kind of jazz: elegant, heady, slightly detached Gil Evans. Now and then one of Calliope's song-chants drifted down from the loft and blended in.

"I love you." Don tenderly kissed Meg. "I want to put my dishpan hands all over your sumptuous body."

"I think Goldilocks is playing in our bed, Papa Bear."

"Five to one, she's asleep," Don countered. "The upstairs chorus seems to have stopped."

They stealthily mounted the ladder. Sure enough, Calliope was out cold, cuddling her beautiful dolls and pig. A shaft of sunlight bathed her face, but her eyes didn't blink.

"I didn't think they napped at this age," Meg said doubtfully.

"Questioning your senses, Mrs. Duncan? In favor of some pundit who probably based his theory about children on experiments with rats? That's not like you."

Meg knelt down beside the futon. In sleep, Calliope was pure cherub; the imp had receded. Some inner power compelled Meg to kiss the soft cheek. She lingered for a moment, inhaling essence of child, then rose, bewildered and self-conscious.

"Don't be embarrassed," Don whispered, leading her toward the ladder. "You're allowed to have hormones. In fact, I've always kind of liked your hormones."

Downstairs Meg gulped huge drafts of cold water, as though to wash away the dangerous sentiments she'd just felt. Had she and Don arrived at a brave new beginning only to have it distorted by biology? Resentment sizzled through her veins.

"Don't fight it, don't fight anything," Don said, searing her with a kiss that burned away rational thought.

"Don, this is crazy," she protested dizzily as his hands went to her breasts. But her body wasn't protesting. It was as though the sensual excesses of that morning and the previous night had only served to whet her appetite for more. And somehow her response to the sleeping Calliope keyed into her very center and made her want Don on some exalted level previously unexplored. She wove demanding fingers through his hair and licked the salt from his neck.

She heard a noise and started. "Oh God, I think that's Calliope."

Don pointed to the window. A police launch was chugging by, roiling the bright blue water. "That's what you heard, me hearty. The music of life on the briny deep."

Not satisfied, Meg went up the ladder again. One of Calliope's dolls had slipped off the futon and was staring reproachfully at the ceiling, but the live doll slept on.

Meg descended to find that Don had stripped to the scarlet bikini briefs she'd given him as a valentine back in the land of winter.

She puckered her lips and produced a wolf whistle. "You're some hunk," she said throatily. She let her eyes travel the lean length of him, dwelling on the sculpted muscles, the tendrils of brown hair curling damply on his chest. His body had acquired a fresh patina of gold in their hour by the pool. He looked young, fit, free, in tune with the world, wondrously alive. Her fingertips tingled with the need to stroke him. Her lips swelled with the longing to pay homage to the splendors she beheld.

"Take off your clothes, my darling," Don commanded gently. "It's been hours since I've seen that gorgeous flesh."

Smiling slightly, Meg shook her head. "This one is for you. I want to pleasure you. I want to serve you," she said, the words tasting hot. "A wife's privilege."

"You're being selfish," Don chided. "I want it to be good for you. I want to drive you out of your mind with ecstasy." His hands danced suggestively through the torrid air. His lips parted hungrily. "A husband's right."

Meg took a step closer. "Later. I want to spend the rest of the day thinking about what's coming to me tonight. And I want you to think about what's coming to you right now."

A moan escaped him as Meg knelt in front of him and flicked her tongue across his thighs. "Meg," he cried softly. "Meg."

"I love you," she murmured against his warm skin, nipping gently with her teeth then soothing with the softest kisses. Her tongue traced wider and wider circles on his thighs.

"My knees are going to buckle, damn you." He groaned, pleasure etching his voice.

"You haven't felt anything yet." Her tongue climbed higher; her hands reached up to take hold of Don's red briefs.

"Mama," called a voice from above.

Meg and Don flew apart.

"Mama," came the voice again, more insistent this time.

"What on earth?" Meg began.

"Someone's calling you, Mother dear." Don grabbed her for a teasing kiss.

Meg spun angrily away.

Another "Mama" floated down, too piteous to be ignored.

"She must be having a bad dream," Meg muttered. She started toward the ladder. She felt waves of hurt coming from Don, but she couldn't deal with his pain. Her gut was in an uproar, and a sour taste was taking over her mouth. This time the sea was not to blame.

"I'll just go take a cold shower," Don said behind her. His voice sounded as though it had already passed through ice.

She found Calliope's eyelids trembling in the rapid rhythms of the dream state. She took small satisfaction from having guessed what was going on.

"Meg is here, baby," she said. She sank down onto the futon and stroked buttery blond hair back from the damp forehead.

The eyes opened wide, blinked twice, then signaled recognition. The corners of the rosebud mouth lifted in a smile.

"Hi, Mama Fish," Calliope said. "I was having the awfulest dream."

Guiltily, Meg remembered that she'd gone along with being matriarch of the fabulous Fish clan. She shouldn't have turned on Don the way she had, not seconds after sharing a heady, intimate moment.

But he shouldn't have been so quick to transform her from courtesan to earth mother, damn it!

Then again . . .

Her mind batted verbal Ping-Pong balls at itself, like prosecutor and defense attorney in some interminable trial.

"I dreamed I was drowning and no one was there to save me," Calliope's little hands, sticky from lunch, pawed at Meg. "Because you and Papa Fish were playing backgammon with Jorge and Melinda and my real parents were a million miles away."

"Melinda and Jorge are your real parents," Meg said gently. "And they would never let you drown. None of us would. Baby fishies never drown—didn't you tell me that yourself?"

"Can we swim again this afternoon?"

"Well, not today," Meg said. "We've got to get you back to your parents."

"I'm a princess from a far-away country and my parents are the king and queen," Calliope said dreamily. "Melinda and Jorge are just taking care of me until my real parents can come get me."

Meg turned away to hide her sudden tears. As a child she'd had similar fantasies. It wasn't until her parents were killed that she'd realized how deeply linked they all were. If it hadn't been for Uncle Win's love and rollicking humor, she might never have been happy again.

"Can you teach Maria and Antonio and Salsicha how to swim?" Calliope was asking.

Meg forced a smile and surreptitiously wiped her eyes. "Oh, they're much too formally dressed. But if you can get them swim togs, I will." Meg trusted that was the end of that; the carved wooden creatures deserved to be kept high and dry, saved for Calliope's adulthood.

A while later Meg and Don drove Calliope back to the Sea Grape Lodge in their air-conditioned station wagon. Meg expected Calliope to stick up her nose at the unsleek gray vehicle, so different from the flashy red bullet her parents drove. But the child was enchanted by its large size and by the crisp clicks the seat belts made. Meg inwardly shook her head at the thought of parents whose offspring considered it a rare privilege to observe a fundamental safety rule.

Calliope chattered as they drove across the island, filling up the chilly silence between Meg and Don.

Melinda and Jorge Figueiro were positioned at opposite sides of a backgammon board on one of Pooh Albury's noble wicker couches. They gave Calliope brief kisses and suggested she have a nap; they were all going out to dinner at Marker 88, a good hour-and-a-half drive away.

Calliope kicked the wicker couch. "I already had a nap. I hate the Marker Eighty-eight. Everything has dumb sauces on it. Meg made me a hamburger."

Melinda's exquisitely made-up face wrinkled in distaste.

Feeling put in the middle, Meg said to Calliope, "Isn't it fun to count all the mile markers between here and eighty-eight?"

"I've already done that." Calliope pouted.

"But I bet you didn't know that marker sixty-three on the right-hand side of the road going north has a stork's nest on top of it," Don challenged.

"Does it really?"

"Cross my heart and hope to die," Don assured the little girl, swooping down for a kiss.

On the way back to their car, Meg asked Don, "Is there really a stork's nest?"

The gleam in his eyes was frosted. "What do you care? You're not interested in birds—and if you believed that storks brought human babies, you'd want to drive by that marker all the faster."

"That's not fair," Meg said in a choked voice, pulling the car door closed on her side.

"Isn't it?" Don started the ignition and turned onto Whitehead Street. "I think it's eminently fair. And for your information, of course the nest is really there. I wouldn't lie to that child. She has enough disappointments in her life."

In brief, formal words they decided to spend the next several hours apart. Meg would check out the shops on Duval, maybe buy a new swimsuit. Don would take the car back to dockside and start unpacking their many duffel bags and boxes.

As she got out of the car on Duval Street, Meg fought back tears. Don's perfunctory kiss had stung more than a slap would have.

# Chapter 10

A WEEK LIMPED BY ABOARD THE AGUALINDA. Meg and Don didn't fight, but they didn't sing, either. Bed was a place to sleep. Talk across their morning coffee centered on the weather and their separate plans for the day.

Meg could think of no parallel time in their marriage. They'd had their share of quarrels, but one of them had always quickly conceded that the other was speaking in the voice of reason. What was happening now was much worse than a quarrel. It had nothing to do with ideas. It was as though they'd stripped to their bare essences, and their essences hopelessly clashed.

Miserably, Meg decided that their marriage had worked all these years because there had been so much separation. Even when she and Don had been posted together, or had been off on vacation, the prospect of separation had always loomed.

Now they were leading separate lives each day—but what a difference. No external demand had put this distance between them; they'd simply pushed each other away. And where was the redeeming sweet anticipation of reunion?

While Don went out in a glass-bottomed boat to explore the Coral

Reef, Meg played landlocked tourist. She submitted to a ride on the Conch Train, a hokey old trolley that tootled through the Key West Historic District to the accompaniment of a nonstop monologue by a red-faced guide who'd said it all too many times before. There was also a boy Calliope's size on the train, further muddling Meg's mind.

She visited the perfectly restored John James Audubon House and marveled at his bird prints; really, birds were more exciting in art than on the wing. But then she saw a bedroom with a fabulous doll's house in it that seemed to be crying out for a child, and she had to run away.

She drank numerous Cuban coffees and key limeades while steeping herself in books filled with local lore. But for every safe page she read, another seemed spring-loaded with danger. One book told her, for instance, that the nickname "Conch" for a native-born Key Wester came from the old custom of putting conch shells on a stick in front of a house where a baby had just been born.

Even the sponge markets, with their cute little seahorse-shaped soaps in bright colors, made her think of cute little people. She finally took refuge in a dim, aromatic back-alley shop where three silent, dark men were making cigars from Cuban seed tobacco—strictly grown-up business.

She seemed a stranger to herself. Not only did she avoid Don's eyes, but she avoided her own eyes in the mirror. Who was the real Meg? Was it the Meg whose heart had kicked up its heels for joy when Calliope had praised her cooking? Or was it the Meg whose heart had felt plain kicked when Don had addressed her as "Mother dear"?

One thing was frighteningly certain. Don, the man she once thought she knew inside out, had somehow been transformed. He'd started with trees and flowers and ended up with babies. Her city fella had become a nature boy, and he wanted her to change along with him: no question. Yet it was—or had been—part of the glory of their marriage that neither had ever asked the other to change.

On the other hand (so many hands!), they'd never demanded of each other that they remain static. And they'd always shared their separate interests. Back in Washington, Don had developed an interest in computer graphics only to have Meg become the greater enthusiast. And she had turned him on to tennis, only to have him become the strong partner. What was it Don had said shortly after they'd arrived in Key West? Things died unless they changed. She felt the truth in that message, scary though it was.

But to think about having a child after ten years of not thinking about having a child—there was a change so enormous as to constitute a virtual reconstruction. There was no doubt in her mind that Don's new thinking had quite remade him. Had he leaped out of their shared world in the course of making this internal leap? Meg walked from one end of Key West to the other, searching for the answer. But resolution seemed beyond her. She felt both flattered and insulted, both honored and betrayed.

She was awakened in the middle of one night by a pain on her lower right side. She lay in the dark, not touching Don, trying to convince herself that the pain was psychosomatic, begging the boat to rock her back to sleep. Don looked questioningly at her haggard face in the morning, but the pain was gone and she didn't say a word. In the midst of their discomfort with each other, it seemed a cheap shot to claim physical illness and beg for sympathy.

The pain came back and didn't go away. Now it seemed more of a game-player's move to hold back the news than to declare it.

"Is it possible to have appendicitis when your appendix is gone?" she asked Don lightly over breakfast.

He wasn't distracted by her deliberate foolishness. "You're hurting, aren't you?" he said bluntly. "I've seen it on your face, but I wasn't going to force you to tell me."

"It's probably nothing," Meg said. She took a big bite of toast as though to announce that her normal, hearty appetite ruled out serious illness. In fact, she'd lost a couple of pounds, judging from the fit of her white cotton pants.

"It could be that you've got some kind of scar tissue build-up from the appendectomy," Don said. "I remember my mother once had trouble with that. She ended up having the scar tissue removed. Want me to cable her?"

Don's parents, retired from their successful mom-and-pop hardware business, were living in the Duncan ancestral village in northern Scotland.

"Oh, why alarm your folks?" Meg said. She felt compelled to add, "It's a bit south of my appendix scar, actually."

Don's face seemed to grow pale. "I don't want to overreact, but aren't there cases of IUD's perforating the uterine wall?"

The look of concern on his face irritated Meg more than it touched her. "I think you'd be less worried if my brain were in danger of being perforated. Let's save that uterus, above all."

"Come on, Meg." Don shook his head in disbelief. Urging lightness into his voice, he added, "You wouldn't be much of a mother with a perforated brain."

Meg let out a sharp breath, not sure whether she was relieved or appalled that the baby issue was finally out in the open. Maybe she was relieved *and* appalled. But, damn it, she was really hurting now— hurting in an insistent physical way she couldn't ignore. Never one to induce anxiety by grilling doctors, and trusting in luck about as much as she did in medicine, she still knew enough about anatomy to know that a perforated uterus was serious stuff. Even if you had no intention of bearing children.

And Win—who'd influenced her thinking about medicine—hadn't done so well for himself by ignoring signals from his body and trusting in luck, not doctors.

"I'll call Ed Roberts," she said, invoking the name of their longtime friend and family physician.

"You don't want to call what's his name—Miller—your gynecologist?"

"Ed," Meg reiterated stiffly. "If he suggests I call Miller, I will. I'll walk up to one of the motels and use a pay phone. Do you have our telephone credit card number? I think I lost my card."

Don extracted the card and laid it on the table. "Let me go with you," he said. His hand reached for Meg's.

Meg closed her eyes for an instant, so powerfully did the contact affect her. "Thank you, but I think I'd rather go by myself."

"Thank you!" Don echoed bitterly, withdrawing his hand. "I'm your *husband*. I'm not some passing stranger trying to play Good Samaritan." A muscle worked in his cheek, accentuating the all-American bones in his boyish face. His brown eyes had centers of fire.

Meg's eyes focused for a moment on the perfect straightness of his nose. Would a child of theirs have that nose—or Meg's tip-tilted version? She shook off the ridiculous question, furious at the trickster mind she could no longer call her own.

"I didn't intend to hurt your feelings," she said, meaning the words. "It's just that it will be less emotional for me if I make the phone call myself. It'll seem more routine, or something. But I'll come right back and tell you what Ed says. Bet you a basket of conch fritters the walk to the phone booth cures me, and Ed and I have some laughs." She smiled weakly, not believing for a minute that the pain would simply go away. It was pulsing now, tugging. Her head and the back of her neck were aching, too—a more familiar sort of pain: tension, the sort of tension she and Don had meant to leave behind along with their books and paintings.

She looked around the *Agualinda*, smiling ruefully. Even with all their possessions unpacked, she and Don hadn't really managed to make it look like home. Maybe a good old four-star headache would put their personal stamp on the joint. At least her worst fear about Key West wasn't coming true—the fear that she would become too relaxed, that she would forget to strive.

She stood up. Impulsively she said, "Come with me if it will make you feel better."

"I'm sorry I made you think about *me* at a time like this," Don was saying at the same moment.

They burst into laughter—their first shared merriment in oh, so many days.

"Do come with me," Meg said softly. "For my sake as well as for yours."

The distance between them magically melted. They clutched each other with a fervor reminiscent to Meg of their postseparation reunions of old.

Maybe their chilliness these past few days, the *psychic* distance between them, had been necessary. Maybe they'd trained their bodies and spirits to expect separation, to need it.

As Meg and Don walked up toward El Patio Motel, she gave voice to her thoughts.

"That's as good as any other theory," said Don, who regarded psychology as a very soft science. He put his arm around her. "I don't care how we explain this last week as long as we don't have to relive it. How are you doing, sweet thing? Sure we shouldn't have taken the car?"

"Walking feels good."

They continued in silence for a while, hands linked. Meg thought she'd rather be sick and have things right between her and Don than be well and at war.

They heard a distant rumble of thunder. Don pointed to a layer of storm clouds in the otherwise placid sky and said rain would be coming within the hour.

Meg wondered nervously if they were going to have their first real taste of weather. She'd scarcely noticed the motion on the *Agualinda* the past few days; she'd been too distracted and maybe she finally had her sea legs. But now that she was undistracted, she shuddered at the thought of the rocking and rolling the houseboat would do in a storm.

Don seemed to read her mind. "We can stay on land tonight if you like," he said. "Book a room at the Sea Grape Lodge or up at Casa Marina. Of course, we'll probably get two skinny beds."

Their laughter bounced off a second round of thunder. Meg felt buoyed by the shared private joke. She imagined that her hand was bonded cell-to-cell to Don's hand; and so their souls were bonded.

Meg put through the call from the open-air pay phone near the pool at El Patio Motel. Listening to the sounds of jaunty swimmers, looking at the fantastic palm trees and theatrical Spanish dagger plants, it was hard to think she might be ill. How could anything bad happen to her on this playground of an island?

Ed Roberts was on the phone in an instant, sounding so dear and safe and familiar that tears prickled Meg's eyelids. She chatted long enough to find out that he and Andrea were in great shape, and then she imparted her news.

"Probably nothing much at all," Ed said, "but there's no point in playing it too cool. Could be some minor form of colitis or a fibroid tumor of the ovary. Don't let the word *tumor* scare you—they're benign cysts and they generally go away all by themselves, but there's no need for you to be in discomfort or suspense."

"Do you know any doctors in Key West?" Meg asked.

"No, but didn't your Uncle Win—? Oh, I remember, he thought even less of the profession than you do. Frankly, sweetie, if it were Andrea down there, I'd tell her to pass up the local practitioners and get her fanny up to Miami."

Meg giggled. "Fanny, Doctor? I didn't know they called it that in Gray's Anatomy."

"You should see the words in Gray's Anatomy. It happens that I went to medical school with a marvelous woman who has a family practice in Miami. She can cover all the bases for you—G.I. tract, GYN, the works. Her name is Charlotte Fox. Has an office on Northwest Fourteenth Street, near the big medical complex."

"And near the Dadeland County Jail." Meg laughed. She wondered why the mention of Northwest Fourteenth tickled her memory bank. "I know the neighborhood."

"Good. I'll put Frances back on the line when I get off," Ed said. "She'll give you the telephone number."

"You'd trust Dr. Fox with Andrea?" Meg asked, giving in to a bout of anxiety.

Ed's chuckle rolled down the line. "I'd even trust her with you, my pet. Let me have a word with Don."

"So you can tell him to be nice to me in my last hours? Here he is, Ed. Tons of love to Andrea. We're looking forward to Thanksgiving like crazy. But why don't you come for Labor Day instead? I may not last until Thanksgiving."

"You're going to outlast us all," Ed said crisply. "Or do you mean you're not going to last in Key West?"

"'Bye, dear Ed, and thanks," was all Meg said.

Don and Ed chatted briefly. Then Ed's nurse, Frances, got on the line with Meg and told her how to reach Charlotte Fox. Meg immediately called the Miami office and was given an appointment for the following morning.

The first few fat drops of rain were falling as Meg and Don headed back toward the *Agualinda*.

"Shall we drive up to Miami?" Don suggested. "Or should we fly?" He gazed up at the sky. "Could get socked in here for the rest of the day. Or maybe it's going to blow over."

Meg put a gentle hand on his arm. "Don, I want to go alone."

"Do you?" Some of the old stiffness returned to his voice.

"I miss missing you," Meg burst out. "I need to lie awake in some hotel bed—some ridiculous huge hotel bed—and wonder if you're thinking about me as hard as I'm thinking about you."

"I always am," Don said softly. "It's really only been a month that we've been together like this," he went on. "The time in Washington, and the drive down here, and the ten days we've been leading our carefree island life." The last words came out dripping pain, and Meg flinched.

"I'm sorry I haven't been as good at this as I meant to be," she said softly. "I love you so crazily much, Don, and yet—I'm afraid, some- how. I feel off-balance, out of control."

"We've had a lifetime worth of being in control," he said. "Being in control of our emotions, anyway. Now we're truly in charge of our destinies, and I think it's time to relinquish that other control."

"Including birth control?" Meg said. The rain was coming faster now, but it seemed to evaporate the instant it touched her hot skin. She breathed in the good smell.

"Yes," Don agreed. He paused, then said, "Maybe this is a low blow, but it was hearing you talk about Calliope, then seeing you with her that made me want to have a child of our own."

"I don't get it." Meg shook her head, then tasted the spice of her shampoo as the rain streamed down her face in earnest. Impatiently wiping away the wetness, she said, "I wasn't so great with her. I felt self- conscious as hell half the time. Believe me, when she grabbed my skirt with her sticky little hands, I didn't exactly overflow with maternal juices. I just wanted her to let go."

"Oh, you'll never be a madonna." Don chuckled. "I think that's what tickled me so much. You made her feel comfortable without really making any effort, without becoming a different person. I think I real- ized for the first time that no matter how much motherhood would change you, on one level it wouldn't change you at all. You weren't about to become all saccharine and cutesy-poo, nothing but peanut butter on your mind. You would still be a grown-up. You would still belong to me first of all."

Reaching the dock just as the cloud let loose, they dashed down to the *Agualinda*. Inside, Meg went for towels while Don reached for the pure malt whiskey and poured each of them a tot from the triangular bottle.

"Ed would say it's necessary medicine after that soaking," Don said, looking guiltily at the clock: not yet noon.

"Anyway, it's the cocktail hour in Scotland," Meg contributed.

"Your health," Don said with sudden gravity. He raised his glass.

"To yours," Meg returned, taking a small sip of the smoky Scotch. "Well, there's no point in standing around in wet clothes." She took another sip, then set down her glass and unbuttoned her navy-and-white shirt.

"No point at all," Don agreed. He pulled off his short-sleeved polo shirt. "Why do I suddenly want you so much?" he asked, a lazy smile starting across his face.

"Why shouldn't you want me? I want you." Meg stepped out of her white cotton pants. She preened a bit, showing off her delicately embroidered handkerchief-thin cotton bra and bikini panties.

"Delicious," Don murmured. He took a step toward her, then stopped. "Do we dare?"

"Because of my mysterious ailment, you mean?" Meg laughed. "It's safely out of the line of fire, I think. I can't even feel it at the moment. I think it's one of those benevolent tumors Ed talked about—and it went away all by itself." When Don didn't move, she threatened, "If I have to take the initiative, I will."

"God, I love you," he said. He closed the distance between them, his arms going around her. Outside there were waves crashing against the hull of the *Agualinda*, but they made a thin noise in Meg's ears next to the pounding of her own blood.

Although the houseboat was fairly steady, they decided not to risk the ladder. Bringing a towel for their sheet, they headed for the love-seat.

No one had to take the initiative. Desire flamed on its own. Union simply *was*. The loveseat lived up to its name. Meg felt loosed from her personal moorings and set adrift on a gorgeous sea.

Afterward, Don said, "I won't be hurt now if you go to Miami on your own. I think I know how much you love me."

"You can't know how much," Meg murmured against his shoulder. "It's beyond all earthly measure."

"And I love you as much."

They slept until midafternoon, when the storm blew away and the sun beamed through their window.

# Chapter 11

M EG DUNCAN LOOKED at the enormous bed and laughed. "The good old law of inverse bed ratios," she said softly into the still air of her room at the Coconut Grove Hotel. She gave the beige bedspread a pat, as if the bed were a co-star in the familiar little drama. But her laughter rang hollow; the words and gesture felt forced.

Catching sight of herself in the mirror opposite the bed, she shook her head. She wasn't being honest with herself. She was glad to be back onstage in the long-running production called *The Duncans Spend a Night Apart, Aching for Each Other*. She just felt guilty about feeling good, as if her pleasure in the ironies of separation and solitude were a betrayal of Don and the marriage.

Then again, maybe she'd played this role once too often.

She turned away from the taunting mirror and coaxed herself into singing the upbeat words to "Fine and Dandy." She set about her usual rituals—putting the photograph of the Duncans' tennis-victory hug on the dresser, spreading her cosmetics about the bathroom she didn't have to share. She took a shower to wash off the stickiness of the plane trip from Key West. She sat on the enormous bed and looked at the telephone.

Don could call her if he wanted to; he'd said he would call to kiss her good night. But she couldn't call him. The best she could do if she needed to talk to him was to leave a message with Flip at the Half Shell. She could even ask Flip to run out to the *Agualinda* in a pinch; but that would be all too reminiscent of the last time she'd stayed at the Coconut Grove, when she'd discovered that her Uncle Win was ill.

Damn disconnection, anyway. What was the good of being away from Don if she couldn't just pick up the phone and say, "Wish you were here"?

She became conscious of the pulsing in her lower right side. But the heaviness in her heart was the larger pain, the greater presence. Something had been wrong in Key West, and she'd thought this jaunt to Miami would cure it. Not with whatever remedy Dr. Fox might prescribe, but with the tried-and-true medicine of a night away on her own. Either she'd misdiagnosed what was wrong, or she'd erred in her choice of treatment. Somehow this dose of separation wasn't going to work.

Oh, well. It wasn't going to be fatal, either. She might as well make the best of it. She would go for a swim, then treat herself to dinner at the glossy Horatio's on top of the hotel tower. She seemed to remember that they did nice things with lobster there. And this time she could test the mettle of their wine list, too, without worrying that she was misspending the taxpayers' dollars.

Emerging at the pool area, she half expected Calliope to come darting out from behind a waving palm. But there were no turquoise eyes flashing mischievously at her; there was only the memory-laden turquoise of the water.

She drove herself to swim lap after lap, alternating crawl and breaststroke, trying to find triumph in having the pool to herself, trying to exult because her pacing was her own.

Pleasantly exhausted, she stretched out on a chaise longue and closed her eyes. She was all but asleep when two male voices pulled her to the surface of consciousness.

"Looks great," one man was saying, "but I don't have time to swim—unless I work through dinner. I've got a hundred-page brief to go through, and that Supreme Court ruling to puzzle out. Who would have expected the Chief to dissent on this one?"

"Well, I'm going to change and swim," the other, deeper, voice said. "After sitting through that meeting, my mind isn't worth a damn."

Even before she opened her eyes, Meg knew what the men would look like. They'd have that lean, hungry air typical of young lawyers. They'd be wearing the khaki or seersucker suits Don had favored for summer in his lawyering days, and Oxford-cloth shirts, striped ties, maroon socks, wing-tipped shoes. Each would have an overstuffed briefcase in hand.

Reality so perfectly dovetailed with her expectations that she flashed the men a wide smile.

"And hello there," the taller one, the one with the deeper voice, said to her. "You're absolutely right, my dear. We should shuck our ridiculous duds and join you. And that's what we're going to do. *I'm* going to, anyway. I'm Mitch Younger, and this workaholic is Pete O'Hanlon. Don't go away."

He was so young, so sure of himself, so somehow innocent beneath the patter, that Meg went on smiling. "I'm Meg Duncan. And I have no intention of going away."

"Meg Duncan!" exclaimed the man who'd been introduced as Pete O'Hanlon. "Maybe you should change it to Maggie. There's a fierce old warhorse of a government lawyer who goes around using your name."

"A lawyer?" Meg echoed, trying to sound faintly scandalized. She turned over to hide the amused expression on her face—and because she saw that her breasts were being subjected to the usual scrutiny.

"Yeah, I know," Mitch Younger said. "An unsuitable profession for a woman. Or a man. Anyone of the human persuasion. At least on a day like today. The Supreme Court is in summer recess, and for the next two hours, so am I. Come on, Pete. You going to pass up the rare opportunity to share a sunbeam with the lovely Ms. Duncan?"

"Maybe the lovely Ms. Duncan will join us for a drink later. I've just got to get through that brief."

Digging at each other, the two men started away.

Meg stared after them, lightning bolts of recognition blazing through the confusion in her brain. Whatever was wrong with her marriage had nothing to do with how much time she spent close to—

or away from—Don. The problem was that she had nothing on her mind but her mind itself!

Stretching catlike on the chaise, she allowed herself the luxury of admitting she was envious of the two young lawyers she'd just met. Frolicking in the water and basking in the sun were tonic when she had a thick, complicated brief awaiting her and a meeting of colleagues facing her the next morning. But without the tang of work to balance the sweetness of indolence, life became—face it, Meg Duncan—a bore.

A freshet of guilt sprang up in the fertile soil of her psyche. Really, she was being too awfully disloyal to Don, and to the memory of Win. She ought to be grateful that she could afford the luxury of lying there in the late afternoon sun, free to stew in her own juices.

Don had more than once called her his Boston puritan, weaned on the work ethic, doomed to feel uneasy unless she was helping to spin the wheels that made the world go around. She riffled deliberately through her memory bank, reminding herself of all the times that her job had seemed tedious and over-demanding. Briefs really did make soporific reading. Meetings so often seemed a waste of time.

Impatiently she grabbed her towel and got up. Attorney Younger was going to be disappointed, but she couldn't stick around. She'd no doubt end up revealing that she was the fierce old warhorse of a government lawyer who bore her name. She'd start talking shop. And she'd end up feeling as though she'd broken a solemn vow she'd exchanged with Don.

Meg went back to her room for a rinse-off and a change, then walked the half-mile to the Coconut Grove shopping area. She would buy herself a mystery novel, she decided. Something with outsize heroes and villains, descriptions of exotic places, and a dense, absorbing, distracting plot.

She selected a classic of international intrigue set against the background of the pro tennis circuit. "The beach book of the year!" proclaimed a blurb on the back. Don would surely approve.

Lingering in town, she admired the tropical prettiness of the pale, low buildings. Here was a community dedicated to endless summer, to the unabashed pursuit of easy pleasures. Every third shop seemed to sell fancy ice cream. Bars, cafes, and boutiques full of frivolous clothes abounded.

Her eye was caught by a silky red bikini on a mannequin in one of the windows. Hadn't Don said he wanted to see her in such a confection? Never mind if she wouldn't dream of wearing it in public. She had all the money in the world. She could afford to buy a bikini for her husband's private delight.

Stripping to her panties, she tried it on. Even in the privacy of the curtained-off dressing room, she blushed. The skimpy bra positively offered up her breasts. Swaying slightly as she studied her reflection in the mirror, she envisioned how Don's eyes would flash gold when he saw her dressed—undressed—like this. Her ears tingled as she imagined the steamy words he would say. Her nipples came to attention, eager for the fervent caresses of his hands, lips, and tongue.

"Good fit?" the glossy young saleswoman called from outside the dressing room.

"Fine. Perfect," Meg said hastily. "I'll take it."

Skipping happily away from the shop with her small package, Meg decided to drop hints about the bikini when Don called to kiss her good night. Let him simmer a little aboard the *Agualinda* that night, while she was tossing and hugging her pillow in her oversized bed.

She went up to her room to drop off the bikini. As if on cue, the telephone started ringing. So Don had been unable to wait for that kiss! She answered with an exuberant hello.

"Hello, yourself!" a male voice returned. Not Don's male voice. "You ducked out on us."

"I think you rang the wrong room," Meg began hopefully.

"Oh, no. Don't try that one," said the unmistakable jolly basso voice of Mitch Younger. "I'd recognize those dulcet tones anywhere. Swimming without you was tolerable, Meg Duncan, but I can't bear the idea of drinking without you. Come join me in the Brasserie. I'll buy you a Bra Burger and all the booze you can drink."

"I'm married," Meg said bluntly, thinking to put an end to his patter.

"Well, if your husband were here, I'd buy for him, too," Mitch Younger returned glibly. "Come on, woman. You gotta eat."

Meg sighed. The man was too good-natured to be offensive, but he was getting tiresome. "Thanks, but no thanks," she said. "I have other plans. Good-bye."

Hanging up, Meg freshened for dinner. She put her new espionage novel in her purse. She let the hotel operator know she was going to Horatio's, in case Don called.

To her surprise, the maître d' remembered her from December. Unlike those of his colleagues who discriminated against solo diners, he offered her one of the best tables in the house, near the windows overlooking Sailboat Bay.

Meg gratefully sipped a frothy margarita while she consulted the menu. Although tempted by the Salmon Grand Prix, she had to honor that craving for lobster, in the form of a mousse.

She opened her book and happily let it take over her mind. Was the third-seeded tennis player from Albania what he seemed to be, or a despicable terrorist planning to turn Wimbledon into Armageddon?

The book was lifted from her hands.

"I've read that one," Mitch Younger was saying, "and I can tell you how it all comes out. In the men's semifinals—"

Meg clapped her hands over her ears. "Don't you dare." Realizing she was only encouraging him, she said bluntly, "Look, counselor, I've stated my case. I'm really not interested in company."

"Then why did you leave word with the operator where you'd be?" He waggled a finger at her.

Meg shook her head in disbelief. The young lawyer was tall, tan, and conventionally good-looking—if a bit too blow-dried and slickly mustachioed for Meg's taste. No doubt there were a dozen women in the Brasserie, a decade younger than Meg and with no taste for solitude, who'd be thrilled by his attentions. Why was he pursuing her so avidly? Don might regard her as the most glorious woman in the world, but she could hardly believe she ignited such a spark in Mitch Younger's heart. Most men who were drawn to her because of her sumptuous bosom gave up after the first rebuff.

Was she really projecting eagerness, as he'd implied? No. At worst she'd been guilty of a neutral friendliness.

Something other than the mating game was going on here. She

decided to stop thinking like an object of pursuit and slipped into her lawyer mode.

"You know I'm that 'fierce old warhorse,' don't you?" she guessed. "Are you in immigration law?"

Instantly the man's wolfish leer gave way to a broad smile of confirmation. "Damn, you're as sharp as Victor told us you were."

The waiter appeared, bearing a half-bottle of Navarro Vineyards Gewurtztraminer and a bucket of ice. Meg scarcely acknowledged him. Recognitions were rapidly falling into place. Like Dr. Charlotte Fox, Victor Green had an office on Northwest Fourteenth Street, ten minutes away. Had she subconsciously linked him with the Coconut Grove Hotel because Calliope's parents—obviously his clients—had stayed there? No doubt Mitch Younger and Pete O'Hanlon were at the hotel for a surreptitious late night or early morning meeting with clients.

She gave a resigned sigh.

"You don't like the wine, madame?" the waiter asked.

"No, it's fine. Delicious," Meg said hastily. And it *was* delicious, now that she allowed it to register: crisp and spicy.

If only everything in life were as susceptible to easy judgment as that bottle of wine.

She thought about Don. She thought about Win. She thought about the law. She thought about being true to one's love and being true to oneself.

Her heart was hammering in her ears.

She asked the waiter to bring a second wineglass. She invited Mitch Younger to sit down.

# Chapter 12

Meg writhed with guilt on the enormous bed.

The feathery lobster mousse was a concrete lump in her stomach. The fine wine was acid etching away at her core. She was shivering and perspiring at once, as though beset by some awful tropical fever, and no adjustment of the air-conditioner controls soothed her personal thermostat.

She stared at the telephone, longing for it to ring, dreading that it would ring.

How would she begin their conversation? "Hello, darling . . . I betrayed you tonight." Or maybe, "Hi, sweetie. The weather good? I just broke my vow to you."

Burying her face in her pillow and screwing her eyes shut failed to bring the hoped-for relief. Her infidelity was a film loop, scheduled to run in the theater of her mind for eternity.

*Kawakita v. U.S. . . . Matter of Picone . . . Sadi v. U.S.* The names of the various landmark legal cases she'd discussed with Mitch Younger were a relentless, taunting soundtrack in her ears.

If she and Mitch had physically embraced and exchanged words of endearment and desire, she didn't think she could feel more haunted.

A dry little laugh escaped her lips. Really, Mitch had been almost insultingly quick to abandon his seductive patter. He'd larded their lusty legal discussions with loving words about his marine biologist wife. He'd regaled Meg with pictures of their year-old twins.

It was Meg's mind he had wanted to rub against; and, God, she'd loved every minute.

"Oh, Don," she cried brokenly, "it's what I am. I'm a woman and your wife and your lover first of all, but I'm a lawyer, too. My mind isn't ready to retire yet. It's been turning on itself because it doesn't have enough to do."

She thought she heard the telephone ring, and she jumped; but it was only the sound of a laden room-service cart jangling its way down the hall.

She looked at her watch. After eleven. In her fevered state it struck her that Don had put off making the call for his good-night kiss because he'd guessed what she was up to. "Don't punish me," she moaned. "I have to be what I am. Oh, God, I need you to love all of me. You fell in love with my mind first. I need to think it still turns you on. Oh, Don, I'm so at sea."

Northwest Fourteenth Street. She'd meant all along to visit Victor Green's office after seeing Charlotte Fox, hadn't she? And Don had guessed. Eleven-fifteen. Eleven-thirty. He'd known why she wanted to make the trip to Miami on her own. He saw his dreams of a new life shattered.

Numbly she wondered if they would ever move the marriage off the crossroads where it now stood. She was dreaming of dominating a courtroom again, uttering persuasive words that would resonate for years to come. Don's dream had her narrowing her vision, focusing all her energy on one small crib.

She'd read about such crises in magazine articles on marriage—articles she'd always scanned with a certain amused detachment. One partner "growing," the other standing still. But growth could be a betrayal, couldn't it? Don had no right to expect her to become a totally different person just because he'd changed.

She thought of her Uncle Win, and fresh tears came. He'd always wanted her to have children. An easy wish for men, she mused bitterly; their immortality assured—without any real work on their part.

It was midnight, and her pain turned to panic. Maybe something had happened to Don. A speeding biker oblivious in the night . . . any number of dire possibilities.

With fresh horror she realized she relished the idea of some misfortune—a small one, dear God, without permanent consequences—having befallen Don. Better a broken leg than a broken heart, whether it was his leg or hers, his heart or hers.

But if he were injured, she would feel it; her skin and bones would echo his pain. No matter how divergent their souls at this moment, their flesh was still one.

Twelve-thirty. He knew. He *knew*.

She dozed fitfully, the lights on, jazz in the air on the Miami affiliate of National Public Radio.

She awoke at six to the tattoo of rain against the windows. A thick gray light filtered into the room. Going to the window, she could barely make out the harbor she'd viewed so clearly the day before. What she saw of the water made her heart thump. The waves were slapping into each other, sending up an angry froth.

Oh heaven, what kind of night had it been on the *Agualinda*? She clapped her hands over her ears to shut out the dreadful sounds she imagined—a banging and cracking as the houseboat came loose from its moorings and was thrust by an angry sea against the concrete pilings of the dock.

"Don," she moaned softly. Hurriedly she turned off the radio, which was now giving the national news, and flipped the dial on the cable TV.

A cheery-looking woman with masses of dark hair was standing in front of a weather map. "It's raining in Miami," she said brilliantly, "and showers are expected to continue throughout the day. Temperatures will be in the mid to high eighties. A partial clearing is expected this evening. Tomorrow will be hot and humid, with temperatures well into the nineties."

"Come on, lady," Meg said impatiently.

"For those of you contemplating a weekend in the Keys, the good news is that the National Weather Service has canceled its hurricane advisory for Punta Gorda through Key Largo. Tropical storm Edward weakened as it crossed a persistent upper-level trough in the eastern Caribbean. Isn't that just like a man? However, last night's severe thunderstorms caused considerable flooding, particularly in the middle Keys. Key West continues to report power outages, with approximately two thousand Florida Gas and Electric customers affected. Please, don't open that refrigerator unless you have to! Southern Bell says telephone service has been restored to all parts of Key West except Stock Island. I'll be back with more weekend weather after a look at sports. Are you there, Jack?"

Jack, a redhead in a madras sport coat, was only there for a second before Meg turned him off.

Emotions swept across her body in a storm surge. Relief and anxiety were twin tempests, crowning an undertow of guilt.

The telephone rang, beautiful music drowning out the static in her head.

"Will you settle for a good-morning kiss?" inquired the voice she most loved in the world.

"Dearest darling. Was it a ghastly night?"

Don chuckled softly. "Thank God you heard the news. I decided I preferred the image of you fretting over the weather than thinking I'd drunk one too many at the Half Shell and thrown away my last dime."

Meg shook her head in amazement. How similarly their thoughts ran, even at this time of a fundamental divide. "In fact, I didn't hear the news until a little while ago. But I got through the night with consoling images of you lying in the hospital after a motorcycle hit you— causing only minor injuries, of course."

"Of course."

"How's our houseboat sweet houseboat?" To Meg's surprise, she felt genuine concern.

"I haven't been there yet. Flip heard the storm advisory and warned me to spend the night in something stationary. I threw myself on the mercy of Pooh Albury, and she took me in. She's refused to hear any talk of my paying her, so if you run across something that would make a brilliant present, please buy it. And guess what?"

"What?" Meg asked, her heart speeding up a little.

"I had a gigantic bed!"

Laughing, Meg stretched across her own enormous bed, pulling the telephone with her in the time-honored teen-age manner. "Poor sweetie," she murmured, awash in the aura of intimacy.

"And the good news is," Don went on, "I didn't have it all to myself."

"Oh?" Meg said cautiously. Urging lightness into her voice, she tried, "Six teenagers were in town for the International Cheerleading Contest and you were forced against your will to share it with them?"

"Close," Don said. "I was joined at first light—or first grayness—this morning by our darling Calliope, who jumped and twirled and generally carried on enough for any six cheerleaders."

"Ah. Lucky you. So much for the joys of free lodging. Next time may I suggest the Pier House or Casa Marina?"

"How about tonight, and you join me?" Don suggested. "I've got something important to tell you, and—damn, I miss your thighs."

"My thighs?"

"Those nestling-in thighs, those chewy thighs." Don growled with pleasure. "I've spent ten years concentrating on your more obvious charms. Not that I'm done with them, but let's make the next ten years the decade of the thighs."

"That's disbarrable talk, counselor," Meg said, "and I want to hear more of it. But not when you're in Monroe County and I'm in Dade. Don . . ." Her voice faltered.

"What, darling? Are you hurting?"

Meg's fingers pressed the tender place on the right side of her abdomen. "Hardly at all, really. The doctor's going to laugh me out of her office. It's just . . ."

"Just what, my Meg?"

"I'm scared!" she burst out. "About us. I know what you want to tell me tonight. About how wonderful it was to have Calliope jump all over you this morning, and how serious you are about wanting to have a baby, and—oh, God!" To her horror, tears were trickling down her face.

"Meg," came the soothing voice, "don't, darling. I know you hardly slept last night. This isn't the moment for a heavy discussion. You've got enough on your mind."

"More than you know!" Meg burst out. "Last night I ended up talking shop with a lawyer."

"You did, did you? How were his legs?"

"Don't tease me, Don. He was an immigration lawyer. Someone who . . ." Her voice trailed off, then picked up. She had to get the weight off her chest. "Someone who works for Victor Green."

Don replied in a heavy voice. "Last night at the Sea Grape I learned some interesting things about Victor Green. He—"

Abruptly, his voice was cut off.

"Darling?" Meg called down the line. "Don?"

No answer came to her straining ear. She jiggled the buttons.

"Can I help you?" inquired the hotel operator.

"I was talking with Key West," Meg said frantically, "and we were disconnected."

"I'll try to reconnect you. What is the Key West number?"

"I don't know. The call was placed from there. It should be listed under the Sea Grape Lodge on Truman Avenue."

"I'll try to get the number through Key West Information," the operator said. A moment later she reported, "All the circuits are busy. Power was interrupted during the night, and they may still be experiencing difficulties. Please hang up and try your call later."

Meg used up time showering, dressing, watching the morning news. Now she knew the latest in Washington, London, Tel Aviv. But—after speaking with the operator again—not the lower Keys.

She called Room Service and ordered a light breakfast. If Don were somehow able to call back, she'd be right there. And she wouldn't be adding to the confused swirl in her mind by encountering Mitch Younger downstairs.

The rain outside her window seemed to recede. She consoled herself with the thought that Don was safe and not really angry with her. But, oh, how many miles apart they still were in spirit. Don's desire to have them spend a night at Casa Marina only tossed fresh ice onto the chill in her bones. "New settings for new ideas"—that was a favorite theory of his. Every time he'd proposed that their life make a right-angle turn, they'd been in a hotel or at least an unfamiliar restaurant, somewhere far from home.

Meg tried Key West again. No luck. She paced until her coffee and croissant came.

Then it was nine-thirty, and she had to go see Dr. Fox.

# Chapter 13

T HE TWENTY-STORY PROFESSIONAL BUILDING on Northwest Fourteenth was a gleaming white monolith against the halftone sky. Entering the lobby and confronting a massive bank of elevators, Meg felt her lips describe a half-moon smile. She'd thought it an outrageous coincidence, a cruelty on the part of fate, that Charlotte Fox and Victor Green shared a professional address. But judging from the alphabetical roster of names behind the guard's curving desk, half of Miami's doctors and lawyers practiced here.

Meg understood why. Not only was the building convenient to the Cedars of Lebanon-Jackson Memorial Hospital complex and the county jail and concourse, but it also had an ineffably cosmopolitan air. One might be in Washington, New York, any of the world's great cities. Here one would daily find fresh energy and the will to dare.

Entering Dr. Fox's fourteenth-floor suite, Meg was further enchanted by the view of the placid ribbon known as the Miami River. The rain had stopped and the cloud ceiling had lifted, and she could see pleasure crafts under sail, perhaps retreating from a night on sheltered water and heading back to the open sea. There was even—was it possible?—a houseboat or two moored below, if her eyes didn't deceive her. Yes, definitely, there was a small floating cottage that from this vantage looked like a cousin to the *Agualinda*.

"Mama!" a baby cried, tearing into Meg's attention. Ed Roberts had told her Dr. Fox was a family doctor, but she somehow hadn't been prepared for babies. This one was rolling about in a playpen near the receptionist's desk while its mother, apparently, was in with the doctor. The receptionist, a grandmotherly sort, calmed it by retrieving a toy it had flung through the bars of the playpen. Meg had to admit it was cute as babies went, a little Raggedy Ann of a girl with freckles and wild red hair. And in another five years, when she went to school, the mother—whoever she was—would have her mind back again.

Meg smiled vaguely at an elderly couple in the waiting room, sat down on a smart chrome-and-leather couch, and began filling out the form the receptionist had given her. Name and sex were easy—though for the latter she always mischievously wanted to write "Yes" instead of the proper and predictable "Female." Address: "Aboard the good ship *Lollipop*, somewhere on the briny deep"? She contented herself with listing the post office box they'd acquired along with the *Agualinda*. She even remembered that world's-end-sounding zip code, 33040.

Had she ever suffered from diabetes, heart disease, severe or persistent headaches . . . or any of two dozen other afflictions? She checked off the childhood diseases and then wrote a lot of No's. Have you ever been pregnant? asked the form. She stuck her tongue out at the blue piece of paper. She wrote another, bigger, darker No.

The door to the doctor's inner office opened, and a tall white-haired man appeared, leaning on a cane but smiling broadly. He was followed by an open-faced redheaded woman with a knee-length white lab coat obscuring most of her seersucker skirt.

"Mama!" said the baby in the crib. It pulled itself upright by grasping the bars.

As Meg watched in disbelief, the doctor—it had to be the doctor—bent over the playpen and swung the baby into her arms.

"Mrs. Duncan?" the receptionist said. "Dr. Fox will see you now."

Setting the baby back in the playpen and handing it a cloth picture book, Dr. Fox held out a hand to Meg.

"Ed Roberts called and said you're very special. He also said you're a brilliant lawyer and to be sure not to do anything that could get me sued."

Laughing, instantly liking the woman, Meg said, "Well, I know he thinks the world of you. He made it clear he doesn't think I really need medical attention, but that I shouldn't pass up the chance to get to know you." Looking back at the baby, who was quietly chewing its cloth book, Meg said, "Is that yours?"

"My husband helped," Charlotte Fox said. The pleasant lines around her green eyes crinkled fondly. "In fact, he still helps. I have the baby most mornings, and he has her afternoons. He's a painter, and he loves the morning light, but come noon he's usually worked himself out and is ready to play."

"I'm impressed," Meg said. "Ed didn't tell me you had a child."

"You mean he didn't warn you," Dr. Fox said perceptively, gesturing Meg into the leather armchair opposite her desk. "Actually, it's children, plural. Jeremy is four. He's in day camp. Do you have . . . ?" Scanning Meg's blue form, she said, "I see you don't. Planning to?"

Meg gazed away from the doctor and focused on her walls—the usual array of framed diplomas, flanked by a dozen prints of bright-eyed, bushy-tailed foxes. She smiled at the conceit.

Her smile faded as she answered the doctor's question. "I don't think so. No." Then she blurted out, "I know this must seem rude, but Ed said you went to school together, and—"

"How old am I?" Those friendly crinkle lines appeared again around Charlotte Fox's eyes. "I'm forty-two. Forty-three next month, in fact. I didn't want to be a part-time mother, you see, and it took me a while to learn—mostly from my own patients—that I could combine motherhood and a career. Some days I combine less than brilliantly, but most of the time I manage. More than manage," she added, with a vivid happiness that easily justified the trace of smugness in her voice.

"But weren't you worried—medically, I mean?" Meg said. "It occurred to me the other day, though I didn't tell anyone, of course, that the combined age of my ovaries is seventy." She laughed nervously. "That must sound silly."

"Silly, but understandable," Charlotte Fox said. "Ed mentioned that you play tennis. The combined age of your legs is seventy, but that doesn't keep you from running, I bet."

"And the combined age of our legs when Don and I play doubles is one hundred and forty." Meg laughed. "And we run better together than we do singly. But seriously—"

"But seriously, I had amniocentesis in the fourth month of each pregnancy. That way I was able to be virtually certain that there would be no age-related birth defects. And I had the pleasure of knowing the sex of my children ahead of time," she added. "Some parents who have amniocentesis choose not to be told about the sex, but being in the business—"

"Oh, I'd be the same way," Meg chimed in eagerly. "Don, too, I'm sure. We just couldn't stand the idea of someone knowing something we didn't know about our offspring."

"Exactly. Of course, you might not want to have amnio. Although we technically describe a first-time mother of your age as an elderly primigravida, the incidence of age-related defects doesn't begin to curve steeply until thirty-seven." The telephone rang in the outer office, but the doctor kept her attention fixed firmly on Meg.

"Really?" Staring off into space, Meg murmured, "What I don't know about pregnancy and kids could fill a book. I suppose since I never expected to consider the issue—the *issue* issue—I deliberately steered clear of the topic."

"Yes, knowledge can be very seductive, can't it? And ignorance is a fabulous barrier. Sometimes. Well," the doctor said briskly, "I suppose I ought to take a look at you—though if there's anyone I'd trust to make a diagnosis over the phone, it's Ed Roberts. He's betting on that ovarian cyst. If you'd like to go into Examining Room A and put on a gown, I'll have a look at Mrs. Kantrowitz's goutial toe."

An urgent cry of "Mama" came from the outer office, and Charlotte Fox grinned. Looking at her watch, she commented, "Right on the bell for snack-time." She unself-consciously began to unbutton her smock.

"You mean you manage to nurse the baby?" Meg asked, flabbergasted.

"I'm weaning her now. We're down to two breast-feedings a day; but, yes, I manage. I find it very soothing and refreshing, actually. Sara's much more interested in finger foods than liquids at the moment—she would cheerfully have given up the breast several months ago. I'm the one who welcomes being forced away from my work a couple of times a day. And of course I like showing my OB patients how simple and gratifying nursing is. Examples mean more than even the best of books."

Meg had heard about supermoms, but she'd never met one before; she'd supposed them the invention of magazine editors. Changing out of her clothes and into an examining smock, she all but ripped off a button and realized how angry she was. What kind of funny business had Ed Roberts been up to, sending her to this woman? Ed, who along with Andrea had opted not to have children? True, the Robertses had made their choice for a different reason than Meg and Don; there was a hereditary disorder on both their family trees.

Damn Ed. Damn Charlotte Fox for being so productive and looking so happy. Such a happy-looking baby, too—a baby who would grow up knowing she'd never kept her mother from being her own woman.

For the second time in two days, Meg wondered what a child of hers and Don's would look like. And if they had two, a boy and a girl, they'd have a built-in mixed doubles game for their old age.

Sappy thinking—oh, unbearable thinking. The kind of mush and gush she'd proudly forsworn. But how delicious, how exquisitely sweet the thoughts were.

*No*, she rebelled the next minute, sitting on the side of the examining table and giving it a good kick. She wouldn't be ruled by her biology—she just wouldn't. Her mind ran the show, thank you very much, not her unreliable hormones.

But nursing would be so sensual; it would make some final sense out of those flagrant breasts she'd been endowed with. Would Don be jealous seeing his child's lips where his own loved to be? Lord, no, he would probably adore the sight. In her mind Meg was already urging him to stop at two kids—not even supermom could work with three.

She heaved a great sigh of relief when Charlotte Fox came in and interrupted her internal dialogue. The examination was brief, thorough, and gentle. The doctor's palpating hands confirmed what Ed

Roberts had suspected. Meg had an ovarian cyst about the size of a plum. In all likelihood it would dissolve without ever giving her more than momentary discomfort. But it would have to be observed in another few months. If by chance it grew to the size of an orange, or caused Meg severe pain, simple surgery might be required.

"It stopped hurting already," Meg said. "Just knowing that it's nothing serious seems to have stopped the pain."

"That's usually the case," the doctor said.

"If I wanted . . ." Meg began, then let her voice trail off.

"If you wanted?" the doctor prompted.

"If I wanted to get pregnant, would the cyst interfere?" Meg said all in a rush.

"No," Charlotte Fox replied. "But," she added gravely, "your IUD surely would."

"Take it out," Meg said softly.

The other woman raised her broad, bright eyebrows.

"Take out my IUD," Meg repeated. "Please."

"Just like that?"

"This can't be your first such request," Meg said dryly. "You do a very rousing job of waving the flag for motherhood."

"Meg—may I call you Meg?—and you must call me Charlotte— you have every right to say those words. But the banner I wave is for thought-out parenthood. Believe me, I'm all too happy to dispense with birth-control devices. But I've treated too many battered children to think that childbirth changes psyches. People who aren't eager for children before the fact are rarely good with them after the fact."

Meg's mind flashed to Calliope and her parents. Had she been wanted, and was she now? Somehow Meg had to know.

"You think about that IUD," the doctor went on. "Talk it over with your husband. Be the rational woman you are."

"I want it out now," Meg said in small voice she scarcely recognized as her own, "and I know it's a real and true wanting—and I'm scared that if the deed isn't done, all my fears will come rushing back, my old mindset will take over, and that will forever be that. Believe me, my husband would only be ecstatic."

"Come back in a week," Charlotte said. "Come back tomorrow. I'd be failing you as a doctor and a friend if I listened to you now. A child is forever, Meg Duncan. Not for the period of pregnancy, or birth, or nursing—but forever."

Reluctantly Meg got down off the examining table. "What you don't see, because I didn't see it myself until now, is that I've been making this decision for years. Don and I both have. We just didn't know it. I didn't, anyway. I think he's known for a while."

"Then you'll both still know tomorrow." Charlotte scribbled a notation on Meg's new record.

"You see, there's no such thing as standing still." Meg nodded for emphasis. "If you don't change, you die. If relationships don't change, they die."

"But change for its own sake isn't enough, is it?" Charlotte probed gently.

"Of course not. Change for its own sake just brings chaos and terror. That's what I thought was going on between Don and me, from the moment we set foot on our houseboat. But that's a story for another day. Maybe we can meet for lunch sometime. Does your schedule allow for lunch?"

"It demands lunch. Doctor's orders. Let's do it soon. Whatever you decide about the IUD."

"Oh, I've decided," Meg said. "I'm just waiting for you to catch up."

The women laughed together. Meg felt that they parted real friends.

# Chapter 14

D on—"

"Meg—"

Their voices met in midair as their hands clasped across the table. They were sitting on the patio at the edge of the sea behind the Casa Marina, the great old resort that did for the ocean side of Key West what the Pier House did for the Gulf.

"You go first," Meg said. "You look as though you're going to burst."

He also looked exceptionally handsome, Meg thought. As a concession to the grandeur of the setting, or perhaps because tonight seemed to be an occasion, he was wearing a white linen suit that showed off his polished tan. The navy shirt and red-and-blue tie he'd chosen added drama to his looks. And his hair had grown rakishly long, she realized, perceiving him through eyes opened wide by a day's absence. The hair at the back of his neck seemed to wave where it grazed his collar. He'd taken a brush, or maybe even a blower, to the shock that usually flopped over his forehead and had somehow persuaded it to stay slicked back. She had no doubt that the beach-boy look would return the next morning, cutoff jeans and windblown hair and all. And she'd be glad to see it again. But for the time and the place and the resonant air between them, he was a portrait of the man she wanted him to be.

She was glad she'd gone back to the boutique in Coconut Grove where she'd bought the red bikini and acquired a smashing dress. Hunter-green cotton, almost starchy in its crispness, it had a low square neckline and puffy sleeves, making much of the bosom she usually tried to conceal. The wide belt and green-and-white stripes showed off her slender middle and pared-down hips. Soon enough the waistline would go—at least for a while—as she prepared to be the eternal broad-hipped mother.

"You're exceptionally lovely tonight," Don murmured. "That's a very fine dress."

"I have another recent acquisition to show you," Meg said, meaning the silky, scanty red bikini. "In private."

"Oh? I feel as though we should be in private now." Don leaned forward conspiratorially. "I'm damned tempted to thrust my hand down that inviting neckline."

"Go ahead," Meg dared him. Above her head the great leaves of a coconut palm rustled concurrence with the challenge. Most of the serious drinkers were inside, where the air conditioning was. The few other people on the patio were still in swim clothes and were gathered near the pool.

Don smiled mysteriously. He leaned back for a moment, his hands in his pockets now, seemingly drinking in the sight of Meg and working up the courage to put a hand where his eyes were hotly focused.

Really, she couldn't feel more *touched* than she did now, Meg thought, her nipples stinging sweetly as they stiffened beneath the crisp dress. His eyes were two brands, imprinting her with his logo wrought in golden fire.

Then, casual as anything, he snaked his hand through the air and insinuated it down her cleavage. Meg felt something cold against her pulsing breasts and she gave a little yelp.

"Ice!" she accused.

Don shook his head. "I never repeat my jokes." Withdrawing his hand from the warm, fragrant valley, he showed her a diamond and coral ring.

"For me?" Meg asked, dizzy with pleasure.

"I think a woman needs a fresh diamond every decade," Don said. "A re-engagement ring, if you know what I mean. Let's see. Where shall we put it? On the right hand, don't you think?"

"It's beautiful," Meg breathed. The ring was truly a work of art. Twin-cut diamonds were the eyes for a coral snake tinted the delicate, shimmering, fleshy pinks of the conch shell she prized. A garnet—no, a ruby—chip suggested a mouth.

"Not too Key West artsy?" Don asked.

Meg silently shook her head.

"Darling, listen," Don began. "I bought the ring a couple of weeks ago and tucked it away for the right moment. So please don't think I'm trying to bribe my way back into your favor. I owe you a deep apology."

Meg's heart hammered. Was Don—it wasn't possible, was it?— going to confess some sexual infidelity? Jane Albury? But Jane was a friend. Or was she more eighteen and given to barely-there clothes than she was the loyal and good person she seemed to be.

"It's the baby business." Don gazed intently at her. "I got totally carried away. You were right—I never should have started in with *Ixora fulgens* and all that jazz. I wanted to shuck off my city self. I wanted to see you shuck off yours. But I carried the notion beyond all reason. I put all that terrible pressure on you to consider having a child. I had no business doing that. It wasn't in our contract."

"Contracts are subject to amendment if both parties agree," Meg said softly.

Don shook his head resolutely. "Agreement is one thing and coercion is another. It was the most shameful move I've made in all the years of our marriage." He tried a grin. "Except maybe for the time I double-faulted against Nick and Kathy Webster in that Labor Day round-robin mixed doubles."

"Oh, Don . . ."

He took her right hand and kissed the finger that bore the new ring. "You know I would never try to buy your forgiveness. But let the ring symbolize a new understanding. A new acceptance of each other as we really are." He grinned ruefully. "There I was, with all my eloquent words about the beauty of change. But in changing myself I tried to force you to change. And that was dead wrong."

Meg's heart was brimming. Don's message of love and acceptance outshone all the diamonds on the earth. And what if she told him that she, too, had changed? That she'd had her moment of recognition in Charlotte Fox's office? A woman *could* be a mother without forfeiting her own mind. She, Meg Duncan, could be a mother. Wanted to be a mother. No longer regarded her biological nature as a kind of tyranny.

If she told him now, would he believe her? Or would he think she was trying to repay his gift of love with a sacrifice of her own?

His bright brown eyes probed her questing face. "Darling, don't think I'm being noble. Believe me, after a rude early morning awakening by our friend Calliope, I began counting the virtues of an all-adult existence." Taking both her hands in his, he added, "We've been happy on our own. We'll go on being happy on our own. It's you I love."

"And I love you," Meg said softly. Suddenly she couldn't bear to be imprisoned by chairs and table. "Let's pay our bill and go for a walk on the beach." As Don signaled the waiter, she stripped off her sandals and put them in her bag.

"It's all right for some," Don grumbled enviously, clearly conscious of his white suit and freshly polished loafers, as Meg dabbled her toes in a tidal pool. He remained where the sand was dry.

Feeling disloyal, Meg joined him, taking his hand. They stood looking out over the endless water. Though they were on the opposite side of the island from the sunset, the sky here had its own kind of richness. Pale blue gave way to cobalt; cobalt gave way to bruisy purple.

"Meg, I'm so glad you're not ill," Don said, bestowing a sudden hug. "Tell me about Charlotte Fox. You really didn't say a word, aside from how pleased you were with her diagnosis."

"Oh, what you'd expect from a friend of Ed's. Sharp, hard-working, opinionated—and incredibly nice." She omitted any mention of Charlotte's supermom side.

"Well, I'm glad we have a medical connection in this part of the world," Don said. "How's that lower right side feeling?"

"Now that I'm not worried about it, I really can't feel a thing."

Drawing breath, she went on. "Charlotte has an office in the same professional tower as Victor Green."

"Does she?" Don said noncommittally. "Did you see him?"

"I—no." She tracked the flight of a seagull, then made herself meet Don's eyes. "But I thought that when I go back to see Charlotte, I might stop in and say hello."

"Why do you have to go back to see Charlotte?"

"Oh," Meg fumbled, "she has to check on the cyst. Make sure it's shrunk to the size of a grape, or something. You said on the phone that you found out something about Victor. Something good?"

Don made a face. "Look, I still don't like the man. I don't like the way he likes you. But what he's doing for Calliope and company turns out to be pretty decent. And he's doing it without publicity."

"What do you mean, you don't like the way he likes me?" Meg cried, homing in on the words that mattered most. "He likes my mind. The way *you* used to."

Don chuckled. "But as you so convincingly assured me, that's because your mind is the only part of you he's been at all intimate with."

Meg made a fist and feinted a one-two punch; Don caught her wrist and pulled her to him, kissing her roughly. Meg closed her eyes and groaned with pleasure as the wind rose up off the sea and misted the air with brine. The wind whipped Don's careful hair around his face, and she raked it back with tender fingers.

Behind them they heard the strains of cocktail music and the rising laughter of a carefree crowd. It sounded very thin to Meg, very far away. Don was her music and her laughter. And if he truly didn't want to be a father—well, that was the way it would be. Oh God, how the world had turned, though. She wanted him to want to be a father as fervently as, just a day ago, she'd prayed for him not to want to be one.

But then she had prayed out of fear, and now she was casting up a prayer born of love: Don, keep growing; you taught me how to do it—darling, don't turn back.

And he was saying, "All right, counselor. Let's test that famous mind of yours."

"All right," Meg said, as if nothing else mattered at the moment.

Taking his hand, she let him set a jaunty pace as they walked along the empty beach.

"Which immediate relatives of a U.S. citizen are granted preferential status if they wish to immigrate?"

"Spouse, child, and parents," Meg returned promptly.

"Any exceptions?" Don paused to pick up a pebble of notable roundness and smoothness.

"Well, a spouse if it was a proxy marriage, sham marriage, or a polygamous or incestuous marriage. Did I get them all?" She smiled at Don, wondering where this was leading, meanwhile feeling a sizzle of pleasure as her mental files produced the requisite answers.

Don faced the water and sent his pebble out into the blueness, skipping from wave to wave.

"How do you *do* that?" Meg asked.

"It's all in the wrist. And in knowing how to choose stones. What about parents? Any parents excluded?"

Meg started to shake her head, then arrested the motion. "Wait a minute." She squeezed her eyes shut, the better to concentrate. "Code of Federal Regulations. Section 204.2. The natural parents of an eligible child admitted to this country as an orphan and then given citizenship. Oh, God," she said, as pieces of a puzzle began to fall together. "Calliope?"

Don looked at her with something like awe. "Damn, you're good. Do you know how good you are?"

"How good I *was*, don't you mean?" Meg said softly. She stared out at the infinite sea. Don didn't answer, and she said, "Tell me about the case."

"A classic, in a way. Calliope was born to a desperately poor couple in Brazil—Maria and Antonio Lo Pinto. Antonio was a woodcarver and unemployed. Maria did housework for a couple named Figueiro. They were the local golden couple—endlessly wealthy, good-looking, government connections, radiant health—but they couldn't have a child."

"And Calliope's parents sold her to them," Meg breathed.

"No, they didn't," Don said. "If they had, they wouldn't be so sympathetic. The Figueiros decided to immigrate to the States.

Mrs. Figueiro—Melinda—was a citizen, the daughter of a former U.S. diplomat stationed in Brazil, so of course her husband had immediate-relative status. Maria and Antonio Lo Pinto begged the Figueiros to take their beloved baby, Calliope, with them and raise the child as their own in the land of milk and honey. They felt that the Figueiros, for all their haughtiness, were sincere in their longing for a child and would lavish love as well as material goods on Calliope. And they were romantics when it came to the United States. They were willing to sacrifice their dearest treasure so their child could grow up in freedom."

Meg's eyes filled with tears. Don put a comforting arm around her.

"You haven't heard the saddest part," he said. "In his loneliness for his daughter, Antonio Lo Pinto went on carving dolls and animals like the ones he'd made for Calliope, and Maria went on making them clothes. They gave the toys away to children in the community. Suddenly they were discovered by the tourists. Next thing you know, an entrepreneur from São Paulo took them under his wing. Overnight they were rich and famous. And it all felt totally empty without their only child.

"Meanwhile, the Figueiros were discovering that parenting wasn't their bag. Oh, life with a small baby—and a nanny—had been pleasant enough. But suddenly the baby was a person. She complained incessantly about their nomadic life. She got harder and harder to handle. When Melinda Figueiro read about the Lo Pintos' success in some magazine, she wrote to them asking if they'd like Calliope back."

Meg gasped indignantly. "As if she were an object! I hate those people! I knew the minute I saw them that they had wretched values. Oh, poor Calliope."

"Wait a minute," Don said. "I think it's in their favor that they perceived how much Calliope's natural parents missed her. And I think they had insight into themselves—realized they didn't have the right stuff to be the mother and father Calliope deserved. They didn't mistreat her, remember. They may not have given her an ideal life, but they didn't just leave her behind with servants, or physically abuse her."

"They almost let her drown," Meg retorted, reliving that terrifying day.

"Come on, darling. That sort of near disaster happens with the best of parents."

"Maybe," Meg said, sighing, feeling a new shade of blue. "So where does the law come in? Wait a sec, let me guess." She desperately needed to refocus her mind. "All four grown-ups were in accord about what should be done. The problem was—the U.S. Justice Department. The Lo Pintos didn't want to sacrifice Calliope's opportunity to grow up a U.S. citizen. But the Justice Department wouldn't let them in—because they'd given up their child for adoption. Not only don't they have preferential status, but they're probably regarded with extra suspicion by our dear former employers."

By way of answer, Don took Meg's face in his hands and brought his lips crashing down on hers. His ardent hands gripped her shoulders, then slid down to the intimate contours of her taut, high buttocks and barely there hips.

"I'd forgotten," he whispered into her hair.

"Forgotten what?"

"How much you turn me on when you talk about law. It's as though there's an electronic current between your mind and my body. Which brings us," he added shakily, "to Victor Green. I learned last night that he's representing the Lo Pintos before the Immigration and Naturalization Service—without any fanfare, without any fee. The Figueiros knew him from their travels in fancy Florida circles."

"Everyone travels in circles," Meg heard herself say obscurely. "Victor Green, you, and me. Oh, well. Be that as it may. So he's not so bad after all, is he?"

"Not so bad. And if Pooh Albury thinks enough of him to be planning a wedding—"

"You're kidding!" Meg was delighted. Then her thoughts whirled back to Calliope. "Don, I want to work for him," she blurted out. "I want to work on the Lo Pinto case. I want to work *period*. The first time we met, Victor told me that he and the Justice Department were the flip sides of the same coin. I think he's right, you know. And I want to work on the other side now because I love the system so much. Don't ask me to give up being a mother."

"A lawyer you mean," Don corrected gently.

Meg was grateful that the light of day was all but gone; she felt a hot blush rising in her cheeks.

"A lawyer," she amended.

"The crazy thing," Don said shakily, "is that I realize now how much I've missed your lawyering mind. I didn't want to miss it, but the reality is I did. It's part of what you are. It's a very important thread in the fabric that's us."

"You mean I can work again and you won't feel betrayed?" A surge of wind gusted off the water, and Meg clung to Don.

"I won't feel betrayed. Not even if you work for Victor Green. And if I go on studying subtropical plants? Will that seem a rejection of you?"

The air seemed to clear in Meg's head. "No. That's between you and yourself, isn't it? That's not going to mean you're not my life partner. In life, and for life," she said, her voice tremulous with emotion.

"You're sure?" His hands caressed the back of her neck as he whispered the words in her ear.

"I'm sure. If we do different things during the day—why, we'll be recharged the way we used to be by a different kind of separation. Without," she added, sighing, "having to spend any more nights apart."

"You won't mind coming home in your proper lawyer's clothes and finding me in scruffy jeans?"

Meg fingered the soft fabric of his gleaming white suit jacket. "You won't throw this suit away, will you? You'll still dress like a grown-up now and then?"

"We can go black-tie to the opera," Don said solemnly.

"The opera," Meg said nostalgically. "Is there opera in Key West?" Then she added with a little laugh, "Not that we went so often in Washington. But it was nice knowing it was there."

"Well, if you're going to work for Victor Green, we'll need a home in Miami, too, and Miami has opera. I was thinking about a permanent suite at the Coconut Grove Hotel. At least until we find a house we're crazy about, or find an architect to build one to our specifications."

Meg looked searchingly at her husband. "But you love the *Agualinda*. And what about your tropical plants?"

"If I want to do serious research—and I might—I'm better off there than here. There's a renowned fruit- and spice-tree park on the outskirts of Miami, with specimens from all over the world. And there's the Fairchild Tropical Garden in South Miami."

"You'll end up being the first lawyer in history with trees for clients," Meg said gleefully.

"I just might. Trees have rights. I mean, people are always talking about the roots of law."

Meg swung playfully at him. "That still doesn't take care of the *Agualinda*."

"We can keep it as our retreat. It's been important in our life. And beside," he added with a grin, "Calliope would kill us if we gave it up."

"We could give her and her parents—her real parents—one of Win's other houseboats," Meg said excitedly. "After I win their case."

"The only trouble with you, counselor, is that you have no self-confidence." Don swung her into his arms for a kiss. "God, I love you." His breath was a gentle fire against her cheeks and neck. His lips moved possessively over the warm, tanned skin the green dress offered up, then sought the creamy swells of flesh half-concealed beneath the unyielding cotton. "Love you and want you."

"Now?" Meg gasped, as his fingers found the zipper at her back.

"Now. Here. Look, there's no one around for miles."

Meg did a slow turn of amazement. Sea and sky were all the world. Prickles of light from the Casa Marina and private houses seemed as remote as the twinkling stars. They were too far from the road to hear the traffic as more than a distant murmur. The crash of wave against wave seemed to say that the sea would be their curtain, the sand their bed. That vast black curve of star-spangled sky would be their canopy.

"But your beautiful white suit," Meg demurred.

"And your beautiful green dress. We'll just have to take them off to preserve them."

"We'll be cold," Meg whispered.

"We'll be hot," Don countered. "Are you saying no to me?"

"No. I mean, yes. I mean, no, I'm not saying no, and yes, I'm—"

Her words were cut off as Don's mouth covered her own. A frenzy of kisses hailed down on her lips. She felt her mouth being forced open as Don's tongue searched and invaded. Urgent fingers unfastened her belt; her hips swiveled to hasten the process.

She should have been cold as she stood barefoot on the sand, clad only in the sheerest bra and panties, but Don's smoldering gaze was sun and fire at once. He took a step toward her; she motioned him to stop. She wanted to do her final strip herself, to make an offering of her body. With teasing slowness she reached behind her back to unfasten her bra. She flung the flimsy strip of cloth away, giving an exultant laugh as her bounteous breasts swung free. She let the wind caress her nipples for a dizzying moment, then smiled invitingly at Don.

The moon came out from behind a cloud, giving his face a magical silvery glow as he approached her through the vastness of the night. "Beauty beyond beauty," he murmured. He kissed each nipple in turn, his lips closing over the throbbing flesh. His fingers played imaginary music across the surrounding skin. "Ten years, and I still can't believe they're mine, all mine."

"Yours," Meg hummed into his ear. "They're only beautiful because they're yours." She gave a groan of pure pleasure. "It's so beautiful out here. I love you madly. I feel so free."

"I want to be free too," Don said. He moved away from her long enough to take off his jacket and hand it to her. As he loosened his tie and removed it, she carefully folded his jacket with the lining on the outside and laid it gently on the sand. "So much for spontaneity." Don grinned.

"You want wrinkles?" Meg asked.

"Only on you. And I can wait another few years."

Then he was standing there, naked, and she stepped out of her panties.

Don pulled her into his arms and held her tightly against him. She felt every muscle and hair on his body; she felt his tenderness and desire.

"You know what I want to do?" he whispered. He looped one leg around hers, pinioning an ankle.

"I think I have some idea."

"Something else, I mean. A long-standing fantasy." Don's hands tightened over her hips, then slid behind her to cup her buttocks.

Desire was a liquid flame leaping along Meg's veins. "Anything."

"I want to play tennis with you," Don said.

Meg cocked her head back. "Want to run that by me again?"

"Make-believe tennis. Naked tennis. I want to see the way your breasts rise up when you serve, and the way they bobble when you run to the net when I lob one over." He grabbed up a stick and drew a line. "This will be our net." Grinning sheepishly, he broke out of his fantasy. "Is it too loony?"

"Loony's what we're supposed to be under the lunar spell." Meg pointed up at the mysterious orb of the moon. Suddenly she made a tossing motion. "Rough or smooth?"

"Life with you is both, and both have their place—but I'll take smooth."

Meg bent down to pick up her imaginary racquet. "Smooth it is. Your serve. I guess we don't have to worry about which one of us gets the—er—moony side of the court. I'll play over here. You want to take a few practice shots?"

"First one in," Don called. He crouched behind his imaginary baseline. "You ready?"

"Ready," Meg answered. But she really wasn't ready. As he tossed the ball that wasn't there and arched in the parabola of his serve, she all but grew faint at the vividness of his masculine contours, the sharp delineation of his vital, rugged beauty.

"Fault," she said weakly.

Don crossed his arms over his chest, glared at her, and served the ball again. This time Meg broke out of her adoring reverie and swung. She could have sworn she felt her muscles echo the contact of ball against racquet strings. Following through, she knew she'd returned the ball to the backhand side of Don's baseline—and, yes, he was readying his racquet for a backhand swing. A lob brought her to the net, and he rushed the net, too; and then instead of a ball there was a ravenous kiss.

"Score: love, love," Meg said, when she could speak.

Don put his arms around her. Never before had she felt as she felt on that vast and windy moon-washed beach, that nakedness was the only rightful costume for a man and woman in love. The chief virtue of clothing was that it came off. Part of her needed to be a lawyer, but part would forever need to be the free woman who had surfaced here in Key West.

Thought itself seemed to stop as Don pulled her down to a patch of soft sand. His body hovered over hers, as majestic and eternal as the pounding sea. When he entered her, he brought the moon in with him; and the moon ordained the rising of her personal tide. She rose and fell, and rose and fell again, in accord with the ancient, universal rhythm of the dance of all things male and female.

And, oh God, this should be the union that created a new life; but of course it couldn't be. She felt ungrateful to even be thinking about it, she had so very much, and only the foolish and greedy hoped for everything.

# Chapter 15

P REGNANT?" Meg stared at Charlotte Fox, as disbelieving as if she'd just been told she was growing an extra arm or leg. "But the IUD . . ." she faltered.

"A two percent failure rate," the doctor said briskly. "A small but meaningful statistic—especially if you're a part of it. The good news is that the embryo pushed out the device, so the pregnancy is not at risk." Her green eyes fixed on Meg. "That *is* good news, isn't it?"

"Why, yes, of course," Meg stammered. "How can you ask?"

The doctor made notations on Meg's record. "Because five—no, six—weeks ago, when you first came to see me, you asked me to remove your IUD. I told you to think about it and come back, and you didn't come back. Until you missed a period and thought it had something to do with the cyst."

"I figured it had grown to the size of a watermelon," Meg joked feebly. "In a way the scariest part was that I didn't feel any pain."

"Because the cyst dissolved," Dr. Fox said, a smile wanning her face. "You can get off the examining table now and dress. I think we'll be more comfortable in my office."

Her head spinning as she tried to assimilate the news, Meg put on her shirt and khaki skirt. Caught between ecstasy on her own behalf and dismay on Don's, she felt frozen out from all emotion. Well, at least she could feel unambiguous relief that the cyst was gone, not that it had ever been a serious problem.

As she headed for the doctor's private office, Meg noticed with relief that Charlotte's baby daughter was absent, the playpen folded and put away. Of course: it was afternoon. Sara's father was parent-on-the-spot. For a bittersweet flash of a moment, Meg envisaged Don with Calliope on his shoulders. Oh, why hadn't she leaped to meet him when he tasted the joys of daddyhood and wanted more?

And now fate had made the leap. But how would Don respond? Was it possible that he would want—oh God—not to have it? Questions ricocheted inside her head. How could something so vastly important have happened to her body without her ever knowing?

"But shouldn't I have morning sickness?" Meg asked, as she sat down across from Charlotte's desk.

The other woman laughed tenderly. "You know as much about pregnancy as I do about law. Morning sickness is by no means inevitable."

"Maybe it was getting my sea legs," Meg mumbled. Her eyes filled with tears, and she heard herself telling Charlotte all about her Uncle Win. Then, eager to get away from emotional topics, she said, "It's a good thing I stopped being seasick—never took Dramamine. I don't think I swallowed so much as aspirin this past month, though I do drink a lot of coffee and sometimes wine or a drink in the evening."

"I take it back," Charlotte said. "You do know a thing or two about how to be pregnant. I've written a little pamphlet that will answer some of your questions, and I can recommend other reading. Yes, it would be just as well to give up caffeine and anything more than the occasional drink. You don't smoke, do you?"

"Not since the one I tried when I was sixteen. I'm a tennis player, and I need every bit of my wind."

With sudden blushing insight, Meg intuited that she'd gotten pregnant the night of the wild, naked make-believe tennis game. If ever there had been passion to defeat science, that had been the act. And—quickly calculating her personal rhythms—the time would have been ripe for conception.

Leaving the gleaming white professional building, Meg began to walk aimlessly. Luckily she didn't have a lunch date; she'd planned to spend a couple of hours shopping. She was working for Victor Green three days a week now, and she wanted to beef up her wardrobe. Though she had summer suits from her Washington days, she needed more lightweight outfits to cope with the Miami weather.

Laughing bitterly to herself, she wondered if the Yellow Pages had a special listing: Maternity clothes—working mother. Oh heaven, she could make it all work, the way Charlotte Fox did, if only Don were with her. But she remembered the closed-down look his face had had the day he'd told her he was done with the foolish baby craving and was content with their adults-only life.

Her feet sore, her stomach empty, she wandered into a small Cuban sandwich shop. Ordering a sandwich *especial*, she remembered just in time not to ask for coffee. When she ordered a glass of *leche, por favor*, the dark-haired, heavy set woman on the other side of the counter grinned in complicity and patted her own fertile-looking belly. Meg gave her a nod and a weak smile in return.

As she watched the sandwich being assembled and toasted by a man whose flying hands made the carving of ham and roast pork a matter of the highest artistry, Meg realized what she had to do. She had to stop second-guessing Don's reactions, and present him with the news. It was his news too, after all—his life and his baby as much as hers.

Besides, there really wasn't any question. The baby was here to stay. She savored each delicious bite of the thick, crisp, juicy sandwich, knowing it was helping to nourish a new life.

And if she had to choose between Don and the baby? She covered her eyes, as though darkness could shut out the excruciating thought.

Two mothers came in with infants in carriages. Meg stared for a moment, guessing ages and sexes, then hastily paid the bill and fled.

It was nice to think you could bring babies to restaurants, though. Would Victor let her bring the infant to the office? She remembered that there was some kind of move afoot by a group of mothers to urge employers to set up nurseries in the workplace. Hmm, maybe they needed a lawyer. She imagined herself in a rocker, a little nipper at her breast, law books in her lap. An oddly peaceful picture . . .

A cab driver yelled, "Look where you're going, lady." Instead of yelling back, she asked him to drive her to the Coconut Grove Hotel. Don could drive her back to the professional building later to pick up her car. She was in no condition to be behind the wheel just now.

She expected to find Don by the pool with his pile of horticultural books, but the pool was filled with kids and mothers. Hurrying away from the laughter and splashes, Meg went up to their suite. He was sitting at the desk, staring out the window. Meg thought he looked a little pale in his bright blue swimming trunks.

"Are you okay, sweetie? I thought you'd be at the pool."

"I was." Don smiled absently. Rising, he put his arm around her. "But I just couldn't concentrate. All those kids."

Meg sighed heavily, her fears confirmed.

Suddenly Don burst out, "Meg, I know how you feel about having a baby. But would you consider adopting an older child? Someone already in school so you could go on working? And I could arrange to be there a lot of the time—"

"Don?" Meg just stared at him. "What are you saying?"

"I swore I'd never pressure you again; but, damn it, I can't lie to myself about this any more than you could to yourself about how much you missed the law." Gripping her, he went on: "It tore me apart to see those kids in the pool. All that love to give and receive . . ." His hands dropped to his sides. "Don't hate me for this, darling. But I knew if I didn't tell you what was on my mind, I would begin to resent you. If only—"

Meg shushed him with the tenderest of kisses. "I just saw Charlotte Fox. I don't think we should adopt."

Don reeled as if struck. "Meg, my dearest love. You're not telling me you're ill?"

"No, the cyst has dissolved. I'm in perfect shape. And our baby will be born in May."

Don's golden eyes were as wide as the world. "Our baby?"

Meg felt sobs of joy rising in her throat, but they somehow came out as giggles. "You're a helluva man, Don Duncan. You managed to defeat my IUD."

"The night on the beach," he said instantly. "Oh, the magic of Key

West is real. The conch shell, and the moon . . ." He looked at her face, her breasts, her belly. "I'm not dreaming this? You mean it? You're pregnant—and you want it?"

"Want it so much that I've been in agony for an hour, thinking that you'd changed your mind about fatherhood and the moment for us was lost."

"I just didn't want you to do it for my sake," he said. "Remember that discussion we had once? About how the worst thing in the world would be if either of us said yes to having a child just to make the other one happy?"

"I remember," Meg said. "We were wrong. One thing would have been worse. If we'd both gone on saying no to a child just to make the other happy." Shivering, she added, "If it weren't for the IUD not working, we might never have known."

"Thank heaven for accidents. Thank heaven for everything." Taking her gently by the wrists, Don led Meg through the doorway into the adjoining room. "Thank heaven," he said, starting in on her buttons, "that neither of us is alone with this enormous bed."

# Chapter 16

T HERE WERE SO MANY TOASTS that the Half Shell ran out of champagne, and Flip Peterson had to dash to Captain Hornblower's Grog Shoppe for more.

"To Maria Lo Pinto and Antonio Lo Pinto—United States citizens."

"To Meg Duncan and Don Duncan—it's going to be a girl!"

"To Pooh Albury and Victor Green—happy engagement."

"To Meg and Victor—the best lawyers in the state of Florida."

"To Don for winning a fellowship to study subtropical horticulture at the University of Florida."

"To Andrea Roberts and Ed Roberts—welcome to Key West."

"To Calliope for having a houseboat of her own."

"To Flip for serving the world's best conch fritters."

Meg leaned over her five-month belly to whisper to Don, "And from the looks of things over in that corner, I think we ought to drink to Jane and Flip on the occasion of their first night together."

"Your delicate condition has done nothing to improve your wicked mind," Don whispered back. "Thank God."

Even Melinda and Jorge Figueiro came in for their moment of attention—they were wished a happy trip to Rome and Paris. Meg

KEYS TO THE HEART

found herself aching for them. Now that they'd surrendered Calliope to her natural parents, they seemed to want to cling to the little blond girl. Meg was delighted to hear the Lo Pintos say that Calliope would always have two pairs of parents in addition to themselves—the Figueiros and the Duncans—and there must be many visits.

"And to Win Carruthers who staged this all. We're going to call the baby Winifred."

"She has to have a nickname, Conch-style," Pooh Albury said. "How about Winnie the Pooh?"

"To Key West—where the moon makes true magic."

Later, aboard the *Agualinda*, Meg put her conch shell to her ear and heard a calliope playing.

She snuggled up against Don. "Have we finally done it? Found permanent happiness?"

"I still say there's no such thing—nor should there be. But we have the key to happiness now. We know we'll never be locked out for long. I love you to eternity, Meg."

"No more than I love you." She gave a wide, contented yawn.

"It's not a contest, darling. We're partners, remember? Not opponents."

Putting a tender hand on her blooming belly, he was rewarded by a kick from within.

"Just like her mother. Always has to have the last word." He paused expectantly.

But her mother, still smiling, was fast asleep.